I0650768

THE DEATH MESSENGER
THE COMPLETE CASES OF JIGGER
MASTERS, VOLUME 4

THE DEATH MESSENGER

THE COMPLETE CASES OF JIGGER MASTERS, VOLUME 4

ANTHONY M. RUD

ILLUSTRATED BY
JOSEPH A. FARREN

COVER BY
LEJAREN HILLER

POPULAR PUBLICATIONS · 2025

© 2025 Popular Publications, an imprint of Steeger Properties, LLC

First Edition—2025

PUBLISHING HISTORY

"The Death Messenger" originally appeared in the February/March 1934 issue of *Two-Book Detective* magazine (Vol. 1, No. 4). Copyright © 1934 by Two-Books Magazines, Inc.

"A Giant in the Swimming Pool" originally appeared in the April 21, 1934 issue of *Detective Fiction Weekly* magazine (Vol. 84, No. 2). Copyright © 1934 by The Frank A. Munsey Company. Copyright renewed © 1961 and assigned to Steeger Properties, LLC. All rights reserved.

ALL RIGHTS RESERVED

No part of this book may be reproduced or utilized in any form or by any means without permission in writing from the publisher.

Visit ARGOSYMAGAZINE.COM for more books like this.

TABLE OF CONTENTS

THE DEATH MESSENGER

Once, Twice, Thrice, the Dark Messenger
Struck—and Prepared to Strike Again

1

SNOW WITHOUT TRACKS

NO ONE, LOOKING at the bottom of the shaft, would have imagined that it was out on Long Island, within a hundred miles of New York City itself. The square hole, fifty feet down, was timbered in places like a mine. In other places the earth showed through, wet and glistening. Granite and gravel studded the wetter, blacker earth. A bright nitrogen lamp illuminated the place, and a ladder led upward to the surface above.

But the man crouched at the bottom of the shaft was even more surprising than the hole in the earth. He was dressed in dirty overalls, rubber boots, and a sweatshirt. But a black sateen skullcap covered his head, and a black spade beard covered his chin and cheeks to the cheekbones.

These cheekbones were high and prominent. With his large bulbous nose they gave the man a grotesque, eery appearance.

And the object which engaged the man's attention was more amazing still. It was a large rubber-rimmed thing like an old phonograph horn which he was holding against the granite sidewall of the shaft as a doctor uses a stethoscope. And that was almost what it was—the "ear" of an extremely delicate electric microphone whose cabinet and jumble of wires rested on the wooden platform at the man's feet. He

might almost have been listening to expected noises in the earth's bowels just as during the war men in torpedo-boat destroyers, at just such similar instruments, listened for the propeller beat of hostile submarines far down in the sea-depths beneath them.

Intently the bowed man, squatting on his campstool, listened. For minutes at a time he moved only the muscles of his chest, in deep, slow breathing. His eyes narrowed more and more in their shadowy sockets.

All at once he winced and jerked the ear-phones from his head. A thin, piercing yowl, such as might have been made by a mad cat, came from the microphone!

Then an excited, shrill voice. "Now the two together!" And forthwith from the loud-speaker built into the microphone cabinet, came a bedlam of noise: mingled screams, spits, and screeching yowls as of two maddened tigers in deadly combat.

With a fierce oath, the bearded man shut off the loud-speaker and dropped his earphones on the cabinet. He raised clenched, hairy fists, shaking them before his face. His eyes widened madly until the whites showed all the way around the blue irises.

"Ach! Ach! Gottverdammter—!" He continued on in a whole string of horrible German oaths.

According to his lights, Peter Unger was entirely justi-fied. With all that terrific noise cutting in, there was no possibility of proceeding with the delicate operation on which he had been engaged.

Peter Unger rose to his feet. Once he had been five feet, ten inches, in height. Now the top of his sateen skullcap was a bare four feet above the soles of his heavy rubber boots. He walked bent forward, like a hunchback. His heavy-muscled arms hung down, fists half-clenched, until they almost touched his toes. It was a grotesque, a horri-

ble deformity, but one which any physician could instantly have diagnosed.

One of Peter Unger's hands reached for the metal rung of the ladder leading upward. He swung himself up, ascending rapidly with a peculiar swaying motion.

Guttural growls came with each muscular effort. Yet even with this extra expenditure of breath, he showed no sign of exertion when he bounced up out of the shaft to the floor of the small, jail-strong log cabin above. Here was pump machinery, electrical apparatus, single jacks, a pile of steel drills, and a few shovels. Every bit of metal was spotless and bright, under the ceiling globe he switched on.

Unbolting the heavy door made of split cedar logs, Unger opened it and plunged out into the gray-white of winter dusk. Flakes of snow as small and dry as flour siftings gave the odd effect of haze.

The cabin from which Peter Unger had stepped was at the foot of a long slope. At the crest, set amid a landscaped group of green fir-trees, was a large, many-winged building of elaborate, ornate construction. Nobody but an American millionaire would have built such a huge mass for a residence, and nobody but a new-rich millionaire would have built it in such ugly magnificence.

But large as Fernycroft Mansion was, only three of its many windows showed the yellow gleam of lights. Those three were at the bottom of the grotesque tower on the north side.

Peter Unger stood glaring up at those lighted squares. When he spoke, it was with an angry, grating snarl.

"Static Browne!"

He pulled shut the door behind him, then waddled on

his bent legs to a larger cabin, some twenty yards distant. In this two-room dwelling he spent all the winter hours he was not down laboring in the shaft.

THE CABIN DOOR was of solid green-painted wood. Upon it was screwed a glass sign, showing phosphorescent letters against a black background. The sign read:

Post CXX Annos Patebo

Entering the living quarters for a matter of seconds, Peter emerged with a long and formidable rifle in his hands. This was a Mannlicher .366 equipped with Zeiss telescopic sights and—more significant still—a ribbed Wurzel silencer!

These were the sights and the silencer Peter Unger once had used, when a sniper in the Austrian army. The rifle was not quite the same, but an even better weapon.

Hunching his shoulders, disdaining even a rest, Peter tensed, as a shadow fell upon one of those narrow, lighted windows atop the tower—up the hill and two hundred yards away. A difficult shot, indeed, but not for Peter Unger....

No more than a dry cough told of the slow-squeezed trigger; yet from the far tower sounded a faint, silvery tinkle of falling glass.

Grunting satisfaction, the man turned and waddled through the door. Methodically then he detached the silencer, cleaned the rifle, and stowed both away in the hollow log of the wall where he kept them hidden. Then he sat down and pulled off his boots, surlily eyeing the house phone on the deal table, expecting it to ring.

He got up then, poked the fire in the brick hearth, tossing on two chunks of cannel coal. Then in sock feet he
waddled to the door, opened it six inches, and peered at
the gray stone mansion.

"*Domus Damnatus!*" he whispered hoarsely. The words
were a curse, full of meaning to him, an initiate.

The distant sound of a door slamming reached him in
the still, cold air. *Ach*, the master would come to investigate
for himself, would he? Peter Unger did not move, but his
eyes slitted, and his spade beard worked back and forth as
if he chewed.

This time he was mistaken. A small figure of a girl came
from the direction of the great house. Unger could not see
her plainly, for the occasional firs, but he knew this was
the foolish, inefficient one, the listless, half-alive Fraulein
Holworth. Called a private secretary, *die Taugenichte!*

Peter Unger saw the girl trudge in her flopping goloshes down the path lined with dwarf silver cedars—shrubs
which had not been trimmed for years.

Sally Holworth was through for the day, going home to
the village. Not a pretty girl, Sally. Not even a pleasant one.
Hopeless, spiritless and rather scrubby. Peter Unger had no
pity for her unhappy lot; only a Teutonic contempt for her
weakness and uselessness. Just another one of those in the
'House of the Damned,' as he termed Chester Braithwaite's
rambling residence.

The black moving figure on the slope suddenly stopped,
appeared to stagger backward! Peter Unger looked more
intently. What had come over the girl? She had raised one
arm to her head. Now a shrill, small cry, quickly silenced,
came to him. Sally Holworth appeared to collapse inwardly,

to become much smaller and shapeless as she fell to the ground.

She moved slightly during the next five seconds. Just once. Then she lay quiet, a small heap of black upon the white snow.

For a full quarter of a minute Peter Unger did not move. His deep-set eyes did not as much as blink. Frowning thoughtfully he stared out at the blank vista of snow and shrubbery, the gloomy hill beyond, the crazy pile of masonry which topped the rise.

Nothing was near the fallen girl, no one. The snow lay untracked as it had fallen, for yards around.

Of a sudden the Austrian's bulbous nose began to wrinkle, then to twitch. He sniffed. His eyes widened from the peering slits. A grinning expression of savagery, almost of exultation, twisted his wide, uneven mouth.

"Blood and death!" he chuckled gloatingly. "The weight of the cross upon a cockleshell! Ah-h!"

Waddling indoors, where the oil-soaked cannel coal burned yellow and red in the brick fireplace, Peter Unger took up the house phone from the table, punching the buzzer button five times.

A calm, pleasant voice answered: "Braithwaite speaking!"

"Ha! Ha!" gratingly chuckled Peter Unger, swaying side-wise in his bent-over position, as if to some slow rhythm of an unknown music. "The smell of blood is in the air! Blood on the snow! Blood in the Tower!"

And he slammed down the receiver on its hook. During ensuing moments, still chuckling in his beard, Peter Unger sat down on his cot and pulled on his boots. He paid no attention at all when the house phone buzzed furiously, time after time.

But Peter Unger had made one slight mistake. There was no blood in the north tower of Fernycroft. Not yet. Up there behind the three lighted windows an odd creature whom men called "Static" Browne, felt of the jagged glass of a broken window, and muttered helplessly to himself.

"Dear, dear! Now how in the world could *that* have happened?"

2

JIGGER MASTERS TAKES A CASE

J.C.K. MASTERS AROSE from the witness chair, walked down to the table behind which sat the prosecuting attorney, and whispered a question.

The attorney nodded. "Be back by two-thirty, Jigger," he warned. "We'll probably finish with you then—or tomorrow morning, anyway."

The tall, lean, dark-haired detective shrugged. His wide mouth twisted in a grin. "I can think of other things I'd rather be doing," he admitted, and strode out of the courtroom, bound for a grill-room, where he could get good beer and sandwiches.

He could have a table there, at which to relax and read the early editions of the afternoon papers. And there was a case going on, far out on the northeast end of Long Island, which intrigued "Jigger" Masters. Though the mysteriously slain girl had been named Holworth, the papers featured the name of Braithwaite. Chester Braithwaite, a millionaire in his early thirties, owned Fernycroft Mansion where the murder had been committed. The dead girl had been his private secretary. He had been the one to find her body in the snow just outside the gray stone residence where Braithwaite lived and worked, and where he kept his strange array of cripples and scientific cranks….

The *World-Telegram* article which Masters read as he munched his sandwich, told of the arrest the week before of one of those queer cripples supported in charity by Braithwaite—a curious, bent-over man named Peter Unger. Unger had been arrested because he claimed to have seen Sally Holworth die. But even an ambitious district attorney could not connect him further with the crime, and he had finally been released. Released to return to his gardener's cottage on the Fernycroft estate.

"H'm-m— Now I wonder could this Braithwaite have been interested somehow in the girl—and in getting her out of the way?" said Masters to himself. "She looks homely and unattractive as the devil, judging by the picture here— but it wouldn't be the first time a rich man has got into trouble over his secretary."

Fernycroft Mansion was one of the odd sights of Long Island. Jigger Masters had often driven by there himself, and knew both its history and that of its owner. It was an isolated, wild and barren spot even in summer, and in winter almost desolate, situated as it was on the northern spit of thinly-inhabited land which terminates to eastward in Orient Point. Approximately one hundred miles from New York City, its nearest railroad station was at Green-port on the Long Island Railroad.

The place was not so tremendous in itself; it was its situation on the top of a high knoll, and the gray stone from which it was built, that gave the impression of vast, rambling size.

Eleven years before, its builder and first owner, the

half-mad architect Anders Krehbiel, had died, and for a long time it had remained untenanted. Then it had been purchased by Braithwaite, a wealthy widower without children, who had turned to philanthropy and scientific experimentation after the early death of his young and charming wife.

Braithwaite had remodeled the interior of Fernycroft, making part of it into a research laboratory. And as if eccentricity went with the house, he had there sheltered and encouraged several men who might have been either impractical geniuses or frankly men with delusions. Also, Masters remembered, there had been at least two well-known men, workers in science, who had availed themselves of Braithwaite's hospitality and had died there, though in both cases the coroner had held that death was indubitably natural.

"Huh! Runs a free boarding-house for scientific cranks, you might say," said Masters, grunting at the recollection.

Having refreshed his memory of the place, Jigger Masters turned back to the newspaper reviews of the tragedy.

ON AN EVENING just eleven days before, according to the paper, Sally Holworth had closed her typewriter desk in the downstairs study of Fernycroft, promptly at her usual quitting time. She had been engaged in typing some technical notes written out for her by her employer, Braithwaite.

That evening she had taken the completed part of her work to Braithwaite's desk in the adjoining room. Her employer himself had been standing at a drafting board, working on a blueprint which was thumbtacked down.

She had left without a word. And the next thing, three

minutes later, the house phone, on Braithwaite's desk had buzzed. Peter Unger, out in the gardener's cottage, had called in to say that an accident had befallen Miss Holworth.

Previous to his arrest, when questioned by Captain Hainey of the New York State Troopers, the gardener had hinted strangely and wildly at a supernatural visitation. Little had been made of his story—except that he sounded insane, and therefore might well have killed the girl, himself. That was why he had been taken into custody.

Braithwaite's story had been both simple and straightforward.

He had left his work, not even stopping to put on a hat or coat. He had run out of the side door facing west, finding it dusk, with an inch of new, dry snow on the walk. The air was filled with a fine haze, like frozen Scotch mist. Underfoot he had seen the faint tracks of Miss Holworth's goloshes. He had followed these.

Out there, perhaps a hundred feet away, Miss Holworth's footprints had ended. Her body lay limply in the snow. With a cry of horror, Braithwaite had run to her, knelt and raised her a little from the ground.

All her face, hair, and one side of her body had been saturated with blood, still warm. However, there was no one in sight anywhere—not even any tracks except those of Braithwaite and the girl herself. But the amazing part was that the girl had not been shot, as Braithwaite had at first thought, remembering that his gardener, Unger, had medals for marksmanship. No—the wound had been made by some sharp-pointed weapon, not a bullet—and yet there was no knife anywhere visible, or any signs of who could have stabbed her, or how!

Braithwaite, believing that the girl was dead, but not sure, had carried her immediately back into the house and then telephoned, first for a doctor, and then for the troopers who had a headquarters nearby at Riverhead.

In spite of all they could do, Sally Holworth had never regained consciousness. It was determined by autopsy, performed shortly after midnight, that she had met her death peculiarly—even for a stab wound.

She had been trudging along when it happened. The pointed and double-edged weapon which caused her death had struck her at an *upward* slant! Penetrating her right cheek at a point just below the cheekbone, it had gone through the roof of her mouth, and up, into her brain! The wound was five inches deep.

Death had not been instantaneous, as she had bled freely. At the inquest, occurring two days later, the Medical Examiner had given it as his opinion that she had lived a minute or two. The jury's verdict, of course, was murder by person or persons unknown—though some of the jurors had cast a fishy eye toward Braithwaite himself, and his wild-eyed gardener.

Light snow, which continued through the night, had made impossible any daylight search for footprints of any trespasser on the estate. But the presence of a stranger seemed improbable. Miss Holworth had absolutely no social life; a weekly movie enjoyed alone, for most part, being the extent of her entertainment. She had only one girl friend who lived in Riverhead, and no beaux at all. The girl friend had not seen or heard from her for several days; and when interviewed, shrugged, and said:

"Sally was always a lonely sort."

As soon as the troopers arrived, too, a thorough search of the grounds had been made with flashlights. No sign of a stranger had appeared. Captain Hainey, of the troopers, had said little, but it was obvious that he regarded the murder as an inside job. Like most ruggedly honest, forthright men, he felt that persons who would dwell in a monstrous, unhealthy-looking architectural mistake like Fernycroft Mansion, convicted themselves thereby of whatever mysterious crimes happened to be lying around loose at the moment. And when one of them, who walked and looked like a twisted hunchback, talked crazily of the girl being crushed by the weight of a blood-red cross….

Sensible Captain Hainey had taken Peter Unger and locked him in a cell, before something further happened.

But now Peter Unger was at large again. Nearly two weeks had dragged by—weeks in which state troopers, and detectives from Riverhead, had questioned everyone. If they had formulated any definite suspicions, they had kept the fact from the newspapers. And ninety miles away, in Jamaica, Queens County, Jigger Masters concentrated on the meager facts, drank Pilsner by the pint, and envied with all his heart the chance for investigation which now seemingly was being muffed by those on the ground. A superb case! One which challenged his every faculty!

"HERE'S A MAN I'd like to have you meet, Chief!"

It was a quiet voice. Masters looked up from his paper, the scowl disappearing. The small man, Barnes, who acted as his helper and sometimes as his secretary, stood there

beside the table. Masters' other assistant, Marshall Vandervoort, and another man of perhaps thirty-two or thir-
ty-three, were with him. Young Vandervoort's gray eyes
sparkled with excitement. The stranger with him stood
immobile. His face was handsome though rather ordinary,
and showed lines of worry.

"Mr. Masters, this is Mr. Chester Braithwaite!" Even
faded little Barnes, who would have been equable in an
earthquake, could not restrain a quiver of something like
exultation.

The detective arose, gripping Braithwaite's proffered
hand—and in those few seconds of contact, of measuring
another man eye to eye, deciding that appearances, at least,
were all in favor of this young millionaire. He had an air of
directness and simplicity; and a longer acquaintance probably would disclose a sense of humor, Masters imagined.

"They warned me that you were busy, probably tied up in
court," said Braithwaite, "but I insisted on coming, anyhow.
You're the man I want. I read all about that last job of
yours—the Kennedy murder—and I have a sort of sinking
feeling that this may turn out to be just as mysterious and
horrible! You've read of it, of course. Can you hazard any
kind of a guess as to what must have occurred?"

Masters grinned. "Unless your Peter Unger is a homicidal maniac, or you yourself, Mr. Braithwaite, cherish a
secret passion for old-maid secretaries," he confessed, "I'm
as much in the dark as the reporters!"

Braithwaite's brow furrowed slightly. "There are some
things I haven't told the papers, naturally," he said, after a
moment of hesitation. "First, as regards Peter Unger. The
man is a living, breathing menace—to real estate!"

"*Real* estate!" echoed Marshall Vandervoort amazedly.

"Exactly," grinned Braithwaite. "I happen to own considerable property here and there on the island. But Peter, if let run wild, would scare away all the tenants of my farms, and possible buyers of my suburban property. That's why I have him out at Fernycroft. Just to keep him safely bottled up and happy in his own hole in the ground.

"He's crazy, of course. Somewhere he got hold of that ancient lie—disproved many times—that the whole of Long Island lies over a big river flowing down from Connecticut, under the Sound. Those old croakers used to say that some day the shell of the island would cave in. You've heard that, of course. Well, Unger has resurrected all that, and coupled it with some mediaeval nonsense regarding a bloody cross, and the '*waters under the earth,*' as he calls them—"

"What?" ejaculated Masters. "The— oh, I remember! It was in the paper. *Post CXX Annas Patebo!* A rosy cross! The '*waters under the earth!*' Say, Braithwaite, did you ever hear Unger mention anyone he might see or hear from? Anyone who was dead, perhaps—or had disappeared?"

A peculiar, intent expression came into the millionaire's features. "Say, you *scare* me, Mr. Masters!" he breathed. "What's this all about, anyway? Unger *did* talk about finding someone! How did you guess?"

"Who was it?" countered Jigger Masters, refusing an explanation at the moment.

"It—" began Braithwaite, then stopped with his mouth open. Plainly he had been vastly impressed.

"It was the Swedish match king who committed suicide, Ivar Kreuger!" he finished with a rush.

For a space of heartbeats all four men at the table held their breaths. Then, a peculiar, thin smile on his wide mouth, Jigger Masters got up and paced the length of the grill and back. Then he came back, drew a deep lungful of air, and sat down. He was smiling, but it was the sparkle of hunt-excitement rather than mirth.

"Any time you want, you may write out a check for a retainer, Braithwaite," he said. "I'm taking the case!"

WITH THIS FORMALITY out of the way, Masters settled down to keen questioning of the millionaire. And two items, unknown to the reporters or police, came to light.

First, Chester Braithwaite hoped to marry again soon. He had been paying diligent court to a Miss Sylvia Reese of Easthampton, Long Island. The father of Miss Reese was a minister, and did not think any too highly of rich men. Thus far there had been no definite engagement, though the impetuous and optimistic young suitor had high hopes of the outcome of his suit.

"And the second thing is my work," went on the millionaire. "I have allowed everyone interested to think me an idler. I'm not really that, you know. I have been working alone for over six years on a certain project—something which I think will be a revolutionary innovation in architecture. For a certain reason I do not want news of my plan spread abroad yet, but I will say that it is concerned with a most unusual field of architecture. I must—I simply *must*—finish my design within a few weeks now, and I am badly in need of a helper—a sort of secretary, with good muscles and a certain amount of intelligence. But I suppose that with this tragedy, and all the police running around Fernycroft, I'll never get anyone to come there now."

"Do you want to confide in us the nature of this work of yours?" asked Masters, a tone of heightened respect in his voice.

Braithwaite did. As a matter of fact during ensuing moments, as he leaned forward toward the three listeners, and poured forth his story in a voice quivering with enthusiasm, it was plain to Jigger Masters that the man had actually suffered, by bottling up his secret so long. He was as hungry for appreciation and praise as any starved artist.

Masters finally had to interrupt, gazing briefly at the flyspecked eight-day clock above the bar.

"Due back in court in ten minutes," he said regretfully. "But now, let's go right ahead. I see how my organization can be a help, without waiting until tomorrow for me. Marshall Vandervoort, yours is the first assignment! You are to get a bag of clothes and drive out to Riverhead, and start in making inquiries. This is winter. There aren't many strangers appearing out there for any reason; you'll find three-fourths of all the houses between Riverhead and Orient Point deserted, and the hotels closed. I want to know everything there is to know about any man or woman who has taken up residence out there recently."

"Good!" said young Vandervoort enthusiastically. "I'll go this afternoon."

"And now for yourself, Mr. Braithwaite," concluded Masters, when Vandervoort had shaken hands and vanished, "George Barnes, here, is your new secretary! I can vouch for his complete reliability and intelligence. He may not be up to lifting any heavy weights, but I believe he can help out in your laboratory about as well as you'd expect.

"And the chief thing is, he'll get the 'feel' of Fernycroft!

I want something like a complete history of the servants and your guests out there, and Barnes can get this without creating any disturbance. You can let out that you've engaged him in town, to help with your laboratory work and notes. Don't even mention to the troopers the fact that he is connected with me. I'll have a quiet talk tomorrow with Captain Hainey, whom I know—he and I worked together on the Kennedy case—and I'll square it all with him."

"Well, that will be just excellent!" said Braithwaite warmly. "Does it suit you too, Mr. Barnes?"

The little man's melancholy face lit with a smile. "I've been doing a round of what's left of the night clubs, looking for divorce evidence," he answered indirectly. "A peaceful life at Fernycroft among your maniacs, Mr. Braithwaite, will suit me perfectly!"

3

BLASTING DEATH

BARNES, IN HIS career as assistant to Jigger Masters, had encountered more than a little excitement in his lifetime. But the drive with Braithwaite out Long Island to the millionaire's residence had him gasping for breath. The millionaire drove like a madman, skidding around curves and taking corners on two wheels. Barnes gave a deep breath of relief when they finally rolled up before the sprawling residence on the knoll.

But even here he was not permitted to rest long. After being assigned his room downstairs, and given a hasty pick-up supper, Barnes found himself called to Braithwaite's work-room and plunged immediately into the job of getting acquainted with his future secretarial duties. He had scarcely time to note a few hasty impressions of the strange household whose mysteries he was to investigate.

Braithwaite, the employer, was a far different person here in his double workshop and his big two-story laboratory which occupied a sort of pentagonal apse at the northern rear of Fernycroft. He frothed with the release of energy from high pressure. He dashed back from laboratory to drawing boards, and vice versa. He climbed a ladder, which led up to the scaffolding that surrounded his plastic clay model of a new type of skyscraper. He threw off ideas like a carborundum wheel throws sparks. And the dazzled Barnes had to catch what he could of these red-hot ideas.

In this, as well as in the considerable amount of copying from longhand pages by the unfortunate Miss Holworth, Barnes was handicapped. He knew nothing at all of architecture, but managed to get along fairly well, due to a habit of dogged industry. And he kept his eyes and ears open, noting what he could of these strange oddments of humanity who shared Fernycroft with its owner. He settled down and worked steadily for fifty minutes.

It was perhaps half an hour later that he shifted uneasily and looked around. He would have sworn that someone had entered the room through the doorway at his back—the doorway through which the dead body of Sally Holworth had been taken. But when he whirled, there was no one in sight.

"Damn! Don't tell me I'm getting nerves at my age!" growled Barnes to himself, and pitched into his typing again.

Because of the difficulty of the work, however, such spasms of straightaway accomplishment did not last long. And each time the machine was silent, Barnes found himself listening intently. Something or someone was near, watching him or listening! There could be no mistaking the warning of his sixth sense!

He got up and looked around, even went back to speak to Braithwaite—then thought better of it. The young millionaire was doing something with small oblongs of glass, apparently fixing them into the sides of his clay skyscraper. Windows, perhaps—yet they did not look like windows.

On the way back to the study, Barnes halted in the hall, while prickles attacked the nape of his neck. There *was* someone here!

The little detective could be excused for harboring a tingly chill just then. Other and bigger men had felt much the same the first time they glimpsed the tall, attenuated figure which entered the drawing room through a door-way on the far side.

The man looked enormously tall, framed for an instant there in the door. He was clothed all in black, in what looked like a priest's robe, coming all the way to his feet. The cowl was turned back; and out of it projected a stalk-like neck with protuberant Adam's apple. The neck was dead white, and so long it looked as if it might snap, like a curved crisp stalk of celery. The staring face above it was white, too, and the irregularly dome-shaped skull was egg-like in its baldness.

From a distance he seemed to glide, straight toward Barnes. As he neared the hall, however, the detective saw that he walked with a multitude of mincing, shuffling steps. And he kept both hands and wrists buried in the sleeves of his robe, like a Chinaman!

Barnes had his own share of courage, yet he shrank back, wondering if this weird-looking person might have a knife or other weapon in those flowing sleeves.

No knife appeared, but what did occur was creepy enough. The newcomer shuffled up, sailed on past, lifted one hand and seemed to grope for the stair railing, found it, and then half-turned back toward the mesmerized Barnes.

"You will be sorry! Sorry you ever entered the portals of this house, young man!" he intoned in a resonant, belllike voice. And then, not waiting for an answer, he mounted the staircase slowly and majestically, and disappeared.

"Well, young man, *that* for you!" said Barnes whimsically, wiping the perspiration from his forehead. He had just unobtrusively celebrated his fiftieth birthday the week before, and no sane man could call him "young." He walked back to his typewriter, ruminating.

"Batty! Batty as a barn-owl!" grunted Barnes to himself.

Nevertheless he could not get over the shock of the weird encounter—that and the ever-present sense of being spied upon. Grimly he took out his revolver, looked to make sure it was loaded, and laid it handily near his typewriter. Then he almost jumped out of his chair.

Somewhere a muffled, shrill voice was crying: "Let me out! Let me out, I tell you! It's coming! I— Oh, God, I am innocent! I'm not ready to die!"

Barnes snatched up his revolver, whirled toward the direction of the sound. It had come unmistakably from the big drawing-room outside, almost adjacent to his study. Now it came again but lower, mostly choking gasps, with only a fragmentary word or two of pleading. Then in one hideous, choking shriek, it stopped. A faint hum of resonance hung in the air.

While it lasted, Barnes went swiftly and determinedly in search of the voice. *There was no one in the drawing room!*

In vain he lifted portieres, looked under a lounge, behind chairs, even up the chimney of the broad hearth. He even got on hands and knees and crawled under the big concert grand piano which occupied a dark corner. Nothing!

But then one last groan came, just above his head. He raised involuntarily, jarring himself against the solid piano. Then he scrambled out, and stared blinkingly. There was a rich Javanese tapestry draped over part of the piano. Besides that, however, there was nothing at all save a black leather violin case.

"Fishy!" said Barnes. "Fishy as hell!"

He crawled up where he could take a close look at the violin case. Then he saw it—a thin, all but invisible wire entering the violin case which was not tightly closed. The wire entered the room through a round hole in the baseboard of the wall.

"Oh, yeah—?" grunted Barnes.

He knew a good deal about radio. He opened the violin case, and looked down upon the end of the wire. There was a microphone arrangement there, apparently glued to the rosewood shell of the instrument. The violin, then, had acted as a magnifier and sounding board for the awesome sounds.

"Did you hear it? Do you enjoy man's inhumanity to man?" suddenly demanded a voice behind him.

Barnes whirled. It was the same spectre-looking black-robed individual he had seen before.

"Can't say I'm wild about concerts of that sort," grunted Barnes. "Just what in hell was it, anyhow?"

"Out in Nevada," intoned the newcomer, "a man was legally executed in a lethal cell! You heard him as the gas billowed out at him!"

"My God!" cried Barnes. "Who are *you*, anyway? What kind of monkey-shine do you call this?"

"What? You pretend you have not heard of me? Why, I am Static Browne!"

As if that were sufficient explanation to cover everything, he replaced his long white hands in the sleeves of his robe, and sailed upstairs again.

Barnes stood blinking after him, and then pinched himself surreptitiously. Suddenly he laughed. But he did not attempt any more typing. Just as soon as supper was over, he meant to borrow a car from Braithwaite, drive to Greenport, and there make his long-distance call to Masters. He did not trust this house.

Braithwaite appeared from in back, shedding his smock, and in a hurry. He tossed the information to Barnes that if the trooper, Carey, who had been left to guard the grounds, did not object, he, Braithwaite, was bound over to Easthampton for dinner and the evening. It had been impossible for him to get away to visit Miss Reese during those long, futile days of the coroner's investigation, and Braithwaite was correspondingly anxious. His phone calls to Easthampton had been unsatisfactory to a man in love.

Barnes told the millionaire about his recent amazing encounter with the man who called himself Static Browne, but Braithwaite only laughed. "He's queer but harmless. Used to be a big man in the radio and sound field, but he got his head hurt in an auto accident—and I let him come here to live. His worst habit is that trick of trying to scare people with those hidden microphones of his. But you'll find Dr. Spinelli just as queer in his own way. He's another eccentric scientist I invited out here to live—only his pet hobby is microscope work. Well, I've got to be going. If there's anything you want, just ask for it."

"I was thinking of borrowing a car for a little while—" said Barnes hesitantly.

"Sure! Sure!" said Braithwaite. He fished in his pocket, bringing up a key case. From this he detached a small Yale key. "There are three cars in the garage. This key is for the Chrysler coupé. It hasn't been used much lately. Better take a look at the gas and oil. Pump's in the garage. Oh, and when you get to town, if you do, put in some more alki in the radiator." He tossed out a silver dollar, and turned away hastily to find the State trooper, Carey, who had been left as a guard.

Twenty minutes later Barnes got his derby and overcoat from his small bedroom adjoining his study, and walked out into the blowy, wild night. The little snow which had fallen at the time of the Holworth tragedy had melted. The ground was bare, and slightly frozen. When the sun had been out that day it had thawed, but now crackle ice had formed in the shallow wheel ruts of the bluestone drive.

He was just in time to overhear a fragment of conversation. Peter Unger and Joe Karnett, the mustached janitor, emerged from the garage, and walked past without seeing Barnes.

"I tell you there was somebody there. I saw him!" said Peter Unger in a sullen tone.

"Oh, you and your damn visions!" snarled Joe Karnett. "Whatinell would anybody be doin' out in the garage? Just tell me that now, huh?"

A grunt was the only answer, as the two went on out of hearing.

Had Barnes questioned the pair right then, and made a close examination of his own, it would have been infinitely better for him. The janitor and Unger had found nothing unusual—save a gallon glass bottle, empty, which stood at one side of the garage. Joe Karnett had wondered how that had got there. It probably had held distilled water, the janitor imagined—though he never had heard of any being brought here for the car batteries. These batteries always were serviced in town....

In truth there *had* been an intruder in the garage. He had gone there just as soon as it was pitch dark, and he was no more than a dark blotch, moving in lesser obscurity.

Inside the garage the skulking figure had snapped on an electric torch, shielding the glow carefully with his fingers.

With this much illumination he managed to find the radiator cap of the Chrysler coupé. He handled the full gallon glass bottle gingerly, setting it down as carefully as if it had been the most delicate china.

Then he bent and did something under the front left fender. There came an acrid smell of denatured alcohol, as the radiator anti-freeze mixture drained away. Then the petcock was closed, and the radiator cap unscrewed.

Into the opened top of the cold radiators with infinite care, was poured the contents of the glass bottle. Then the cap went back—but was not screwed. Even that would have been mortally hazardous. The air about now had another odor besides that of alcohol—a sweetish, acrid odor which hung for a moment and then dissipated.

Leaving the empty bottle on the floor near the wall, the dark figure crept out, crouching to the door. A moment of dead silence, listening. Then he crept outside, and the night swallowed him.

Barnes came, climbed into the Chrysler, closed the door,

unlocked the ignition, and set it at ON. Then his feet went to the starter button. He pressed. For a matter of seconds the battery turned the cold motor over sluggishly, as if it would never start.

But it did. At least the spark plug of one cylinder ignited the cold mixture in its cylinder. The ensuing muffled *bang* of gasoline, however, was completely lost in a cataclysm of indescribable, thunderous violence.

The flare of that horrible explosion, which lighted the sullen winter sky, was viewed as far away as Southampton and Sag Harbor. The shock of it rattled dishes in Greenport and Riverhead, miles away. And there at Fernycroft it created havoc comparable only to the sudden opening of a new volcanic crater.

The graystone garage, with all three machines it held, was blown to dust and slivers of wood and metal. The concrete floor was ripped out and a deep excavation left in its place. Every window pane in Fernycroft mansion was smashed, and plaster torn from every wall and ceiling.

A moment later shouts and screams of terror came from Fernycroft. Out at the gardener's cottage sounded the hoarse snarl of Peter Unger, who came limping and waddling, holding his rifle at ready. Far away and mournful, moaned the fire sirens of the neighboring towns, as an alarm was given.

But even when all men who wished to do so came and gazed on the scene of the explosion, all that they found to prove George Barnes had ever been there was a bit of a walnut steering wheel, stained red with blood.

4

CLEAR ALL WIRES!

WITH HIS AUTOMOBILE horn blaring continuously, Jigger Masters roared eastward on the Motor Parkway, the slant-eyed Japanese chauffeur at the wheel bent over, peering into the night like a hawk-eyed Buddha. Eighty… eighty-two… eighty-five miles an hour… underpass and over-pass, almost no cross-roads… whizzing curve and slanting grade… a momentary roughness of asphalt-gravel between ends of the concrete… and all the while the warning yowl of the Klaxon, the rasp of vacuum tires on the road, and the high exuberance of the racing motor.

Jigger Masters slouched beside his chauffeur, Mitsui. He smoked cigarette after cigarette, tossing out the butts through a two-inch aperture at the top of the coupé window. His face showed lined and vengeful. The murder of George Barnes had angered him to the depths of his being. Barnes had been more than an employee, he had been a tried, proven friend.

One thing seemed certain. Someone at Fernycroft must have become suspicious, must have put Barnes out of the way.

But *who?*

"Turn left at Ronkonkoma. Middle Island Road. Have to watch the crossroads then," ordered Masters.

"Can do." The Jap nodded curtly.

Beyond Ronkonkoma the speed diminished somewhat. A little while after that the chauffeur deftly swung the car from the bumpy, rutted peninsular road into the overgrown, neglected grounds of Fernycroft.

A crowd of cars, with all headlights blazing, illumined the scene of tragedy and ruin. Troopers with flashlights were searching every yard of the grounds. A crowd of curious townsfolk from Riverhead, Greenport and the smaller villages, stood about, shivering in the midnight chill—and possibly also with dread of the lurking killer who employed giant explosive.

The first hours of excitement and milling confusion were over. The state troopers and the police detectives from Riverhead were keeping their own counsel, though what they had learned of the tragedy was meager enough. They only knew that the victim was one George Barnes, a secretary—and the *second* secretary to Chester Braithwaite to die through violence, in the short space of two weeks!

They suspected, though, that a giant bomb, perhaps even a huge one, a half-ton airplane bomb, had been let off in the garage. There had been a case, years before, where two of these enormous gravity projectiles had been stolen from the Army air field, at Mineola.

Masters immediately got hold of Captain Hainey, of the troopers, and Braithwaite. They had established a sort of headquarters in the gardener's cottage. Peter Unger, Static Browne, and Dr. Spinelli had been banished to the little cabin over the mine shaft, along with the sharp warning they were not to try to leave. Four uniformed men kept guard over them. Peter Unger himself descended to the bottom of the shaft, where he sat and brooded darkly over the loss of his Mannlicher rifle, which had been taken away from him.

AT SIGHT OF Masters, the visage of Captain Hainey had lighted up.

"Name of Saint Patrick, but it's good to see you, Jigger!" he said, grabbing Masters' hand. "I don't know who sent for you, but you're welcome. Handling troopers is middling easy—but a detective puzzle like this is too deep for my brain! If you'll help us on this, now, like you did on that Kennedy case, I'll be your friend for life!"

Masters smiled. "I'll be glad to help if I can. As a matter of fact Braithwaite, here, had already employed me to investigate Sally Holworth's death. But I'd have come anyway, now. You needn't spread the news, but George Barnes was one of my own men."

"He was *what*—?" Then the trooper captain caught himself. "I'll never tell a soul. But it's too bad about him."

"Whom do you suspect?" inquired Masters grimly.

"I don't know who to suspect. Cripes, half the people at Fernycroft was crazy, so I'm hearing. It might be any one of 'em."

"Well," said Masters, "suppose we start with the few actual facts we know. For one thing, from the smell of the earth out there where the garage stood, I'm pretty sure I can name the explosive. It wasn't T.N.T., cordite, melinite or any of those other high explosives used in Army or Navy bombs. It was dynamite. That is, nitroglycerine—though whether it actually was dynamite, gun-cotton, or plain nitro, will have to be determined otherwise.

"Now, Braithwaite, you said Peter Unger spent a lot of time digging a mine shaft of some kind. Did he have any explosive, do you know?"

"Not to my knowledge. I wouldn't have allowed him to do any blasting. No, there hasn't been any giant powder inside the grounds of Fernycroft ever, as far as I know."

"Then where else can we look for it? Do the farmers around here blast out stumps? Are there gravel pits being opened in the vicinity?"

The millionaire shook his head. "This is just plain waste land. No farms. No gravel pits nearer than Northport, more than halfway back to New York. I haven't heard any blasting out this way for years."

Masters turned to the captain of troopers. "Hainey, you know the Upton Flat Powder Works, of course. About twenty-five miles away. It's been half shut down until just lately, when there's been a sort of cellulose product manufactured there—something like the Du Pont cellophane, I think. Well, I expect they've still got dynamite on hand, if a customer wanted it. Will you please send a competent man over to see if there have been any recent purchases of dynamite—or any thefts. Or if there has been any other nitroglycerine product sold to private parties in the last month."

"I'll get him off first thing in the morning," nodded Hainey.

"All right. Now then, Braithwaite, tell your story. Begin with when you got out here, and what you saw of George Barnes."

The narrative was a plain tale of work on the model skyscraper, with Barnes typing left-over notes. Braithwaite seemed at a loss. He had no suspicions himself of Spinelli or Browne, the two cranks he supported.

"I—I just can't see any connection, why anyone should want to kill my secretaries!" he said helplessly.

"Well, *this* one was a detective, actually on his way to report to me by long-distance phone! You note that he didn't do the obvious thing. He didn't use the phone you have here, and simply have the call put on your bill. Now, what was it he learned from you, Braithwaite, *which gave the murderer cause for alarm?*"

"Good Lord!" cried the millionaire, visibly agitated, "I give you my word, Mr. Masters, I haven't the ghost of an idea! I—to tell the truth, I more than half believed that the bomb was meant for me."

"I see. There is someone who might want to rub you out? Someone with a grudge against you?" asked Masters instantly.

"Grudge? No. I've never harmed anyone, to my knowledge. But just having money and spending it in these times, seems to make some people sore. I've received several hundred cranky or threatening letters in the past four years. Of course I paid no attention to them. But one of those soreheads might have worked up a homicide complex, like that Zangara fellow who shot that Chicago mayor. At least, that was my idea."

"It's possible—but I doubt it. In real life, killer-maniacs give plenty of warning to any impartial observer of their actions. The only trouble is that the signs are not interpreted.

"Now, tell me everything you can think of, in regard to Peter Unger, Static Browne, and Dr. Spinelli. Do you think they might have been afraid a secretary—an outsider, to their minds—might influence you to their disadvantage? Could there have been jealousy over their places in your estimation? Do any of the people here—this Peter Unger, for instance—show an unusual, jealous devotion to you?"

"Unger? He hates me, if anything!" replied the millionaire. "His mind seems as twisted as his body. But to tell the truth, I've noticed very little gratitude or affection on the part of any of them. Not that I expect it. As a matter of fact I keep them around because I find I get a certain inspiration, you might say, out of being charitable. It makes me feel—somehow, superior. And then they do have bright, if odd minds. That also is stimulating."

HE WENT ON to summarize what he knew of the three men.

"Dr. Spinelli was an eminent professor at the University of Rome until he had to leave because of his anti-Mussolini views. And in my opinion, he's a bit hipped on the subject of religion. But he's one of the finest microscopic research scientists in the world. Right now he is engaged in engraving the Bible on a piece of glass about as big as a half-dollar."

"*What?*" gasped Hainey.

"That's right," said Masters, nodding. "I've seen them do it. They use microscopes and engrave the whole map of the United States on the head of a common pin. Of course, it takes a microscope to see it when it is finished. You've told me about Unger. Now this man you call 'Static' Browne—?"

"He used to work in one of the big broadcasting

studios—making the sound effects. Galloping horses, earthquakes, train wrecks—you know. He got hurt in a collision and I brought him here. He experiments all the time with radio—has developed an odd tendency toward practical joking. He scared Sally Holworth out of her chair by hiding a tiny microphone in her desk and making a sound effect like a mouse. And he tried to make your man Barnes believe he had tuned in on a legal execution out in Nevada—they use a gas chamber there, you know—but I gather from Browne that Barnes was too wise to be fooled."

"And what about the others—the servants? Oh, by the way, where were you when the explosion occurred?"

"I was in my room, waiting around to go over to Easthampton. When the garage let go I was lifted right out of my chair. Luckily I wasn't in front of the window. But I was so stunned I couldn't get to my feet, even, for two or three minutes. Every light in the house was put out, and the power lines broken."

"And now, about the servants?"

"The butler, Martin King, is away on a vacation trip; been gone a week. Pierre, the cook, is a real French chef; he gets furious if anyone so much as touches a thing in his kitchen. He was sick tonight, though—in his bed, actually eating his dinner when the explosion took place. Karnett, the janitor and man of all work, you saw. He's a surly individual. His wife, Martha, is very motherly; she keeps house and cooks when Pierre is absent or sick, like tonight. Her daughter, Maudie, serves at table. She's pretty, but dumb. The other maid, Lucy Borden, sleeps at her own home; her brother comes for her at ten every night. All the servants, except Pierre, were eating together in the servants' dining room when the explosion occurred, according to their story. Unless they're all lying, and all in a plot to kill a girl and a man neither of whom had apparently ever done any of them any wrong, I think you'll have to count them out."

Masters stood up. "I'd like to have a talk with Unger and Spinelli and Browne."

Hainey grinned. "I've got them three nuts over there in the next cabin, under guard. I'll have 'em brought right over."

"One at a time, please. But wait—" Jigger rubbed his forehead thoughtfully. "I think I'll just take a look at that place where the girl—Sally Holworth—was killed, first."

The trooper captain looked at him. "You know," he said hesitantly, "I'm probably batty as hell, but I been wonderin' if maybe that girl didn't kill herself. She was homely, never had no boy friends, no fun—and she was kinda sickly, too. Why shouldn't she kill herself? It's damn certain nobody walked up to her and stabbed her, anyway. There weren't any tracks in the snow."

"What could she have done with the weapon, then?" asked Masters. "I understand you searched closely for a considerable distance around."

"Yeah, we did, but we didn't find anything. Want to see the spot? It's pretty well tramped over, now."

"I'd just like to take a look, anyway. Can you show me?"

Hainey nodded. He took a big flashlight and led the way. The spot where Sally Holworth's body had been discovered was some hundred feet distant, on the gravel path leading downhill from the house toward the lake and the village a couple of miles away. On both sides of this path were silver cedars, spaced at intervals, with darker firs behind.

Masters cast about, his steps leading in a widening spiral. After ten minutes he suddenly stopped, peering closely at a branch of cedar. There could be little doubt of it. On the needles was plainly to be seen a red-brown smear!

Blood! And at least twenty feet away from the spot where Sally Holworth had fallen.

Masters pointed it out to Hainey, then carefully cut away the tell-tale branch, telling the captain to wrap it carefully and put it in charge of one of his men. The policeman was dumbfounded, but glad to obey.

"And how does this tie up with your idea, Hainey?" asked the detective. "How did you reconstruct the possibility of suicide? I can't even imagine."

"Oh, prob'ly it's nutty," admitted the captain. "But how about stabbing herself with an icicle? There are some of them hanging right in reach there on the little roof over that side doorway. She come out that way. I've heard of an ice bullet that melted. Well, why couldn't she pick up an icicle as she went out, and then just have an idea, stab herself, break off the thing in the wound—where it'd melt—and then fling the rest of it away as she started to twitch? The other part might have had blood on it and landed in that cedar!"

"That's ingenious," conceded Masters with a dry chuckle. "But I'm afraid no girl, however homely, would be likely to stab herself through the face. Secondly, I doubt that an icicle would pierce the roof of the mouth and the brain. It would be likely to break off too early. No, I'm afraid we will have to find some other explanation. And now let's go back to the cabin."

BRAITHWAITE HAD GONE to have coffee and sandwiches

made. While a trooper went after Static Browne, Masters seized the opportunity to give a last bit of information to the captain.

"By the way, Hainey, I've got young Vandervoort, from my office, out making inquiries concerning possible strangers in the neighborhood. He is motoring around to each village, gossiping, finding out what he can."

"Well," replied Hainey, "I hope he finds out something. But I'm betting we'll find the answer right here on the grounds. If it wasn't suicide, then—Hello, here comes that first nut!"

The trooper sent to the mine shaft cabin had returned, ushering in the tall, gaunt figure of Static Browne. The latter had a blanket-lined tweed overcoat over his black robe, and a knit toque on his head. His pale eyes were staring, expressionless, as he was guided into the cabin and given a chair.

"He's blind," said the trooper apologetically.

"Ah, yes, blind," said Static Browne in his rich, bell-like voice. "But I have compensatory keenness in my other senses. I know there are three men besides myself in this cabin. All of them are tired. They are staring suspiciously at me. I don't care. I have nothing to be afraid of. I hope they will get through with me soon, so I may go to bed."

"Tell us about yourself and your work. How you came to Fernycroft, and what you've done here," said Masters.

"Ah, to be sure. My story is quickly told," nodded the gaunt one. "I have played drums and traps in various orchestras. Late years, before I was robbed of my sight in a bus collision on Riverside Drive, I have been employed in the N.B.C. studios in New York City. For several years

there I collaborated with the production manager in repro-
ducing noises. Very few sounds can be sent over the radio
the way they actually occur in real life. Invariably some
substitute can be found far more realistic than the real
thing. Like the tearing of Bristol board, for the last breaking of a huge tree that starts to topple over. And the dropping of a handful of hairpins into a cigar-box, to imitate
the final crash to earth.

"When I got out of the Neurological Hospital after the
accident, and could not work, Mr. Braithwaite suggested
that I come here. He has been very kind, giving me whatever I wanted to use for sound experiments. I get my little
fun in life dramatizing each new effect I secure—like the
scare I tried to give that poor fellow, Barnes."

A dry chuckle came out of the gaunt throat, though the
muscles of the man's face gave no sign of a smile. Masters
frowned.

"You are totally blind, then, Mr. Browne?"

"Yes, totally. The optic nerve was badly injured. You can
see the scar here." He touched his forehead just above the
thin, irregular nose. A whitish line of scar showed there.

Masters' keen eyes watched the man broodingly as he
responded to questions. According to Browne, however,
there was no reason known to any member of the household why either Sally Holworth or George Barnes should
have been killed. For himself, he never had talked to Sally,
after that one time he had frightened her with the sound
of a mouse gnawing in her typewriter desk.

The encounter with Barnes had meant nothing to
Browne, except as just another practical joke of the sort
he found a peculiarly childish pleasure in.

"Well, there wasn't anything we c'd hold him for," grunted Hainey, as the trooper and Browne departed. Masters had granted permission for the blind man to go back to his own room, and retire there.

"Few murderers would volunteer damaging evidence," said Masters dryly. "I'll tell you one thing, though— Browne is *not* totally blind! His eyes partly closed when he came in the door to face this light. Perhaps he can't see clearly enough to strike with a knife and be sure of his aim; but he can distinguish light from dark."

"The hell!" growled Hainey. "Well, if he's lying about one thing—"

"He's a faker all the way through," said Masters. "That may mean nothing—or a whole lot. We'll see later. Hello, here comes the coffee and sandwiches!" he greeted suddenly, as Braithwaite returned, followed by Karnett, the janitor and all-around man of work. Apparently the servant was in a very grouchy mood, for he dumped his tray down and went out without a word.

Braithwaite shrugged. "Bad tempered brute when he doesn't have his sleep. I'd have got rid of him long ago, except for his wife, the invaluable Martha."

A QUICK ATTACK on the food and coffee was made. Then, with final cups of the steaming liquid before them, and cigarettes lighted, Masters sent for Dr. Spinelli. He came, glaring and highly peevish at the indignity of being kept in a cold hut as a suspect.

"I tell you I know not'ing of any of thees," he snapped, frowning down at Masters and the belligerent Hainey. "I demand you let me alone now. I weesh to go up to my room!"

"Huh!" grunted Hainey, bristling. "We got a nice room with bars on the windows. Maybe you'd like that right off, with no foolin', huh?"

"Never mind, Doctor," said Masters, reassuringly. "I just want to ask you a few preliminary questions. Please sit down."

After a moment's hesitation, Spinelli obeyed. "I tell you, I know not'ing about all thees," he repeated doggedly; but a frightened expression showed for a moment in his black eyes. After a little encouragement from Masters, however, he spoke volubly of himself and his work.

Yes, it was true that he was engraving on glass, using the McEwen micro-writer, which reduces ordinary script to such tiny characters that 3,000 letters appear in the space occupied by an ordinary pencil dot.

"I am not writing so fine as the machine weel write," he confessed. "My Bible, when done, weel take up a whole square inch of glass. It could be written three times in that so-great space!"

In respect to Sally Holworth's death, and the explosion which had killed George Barnes, Spinelli was unable—or unwilling—to help in the least. He scarcely had spoken more than an occasional word of greeting to the girl, and knew nothing except that she took dictation from Braithwaite and did typing for him. Barnes he just had seen for a moment from a distance. Spinelli did, however, make one suggestion which sent shivers up the spine of Jigger Masters.

"Are you so sure thees George Barnes *is* dead? What have you—some blood? Might that not be a rat, out in the garage? I theenk if a man is blown up, some of his bones ought to be found, anyhow." With an inarticulate sound, the detective leapt to his feet. He paced back and forth the width of the small cabin. But then he shook his head.

"Barnes put on his hat and overcoat, and went out to the garage—according to what I was told on the phone before I came, anyhow." He glanced at Hainey, who nodded in corroboration. "A minute later the explosion occurred. Oh, George Barnes was in it, all right. It simply was such a heavy charge of explosive that it destroyed all trace of him.

"But that will be all for now, Dr. Spinelli. Thank you. I'll want a look at your work, through a microscope, one of these days. Oh, yes, if you want to go to bed you can go to your regular room. There will be glass put in the windows by tomorrow night, I think."

For some moments after the Italian had departed, Masters walked slowly up and down, hands clasped behind his back, ignoring the questioning looks of Braithwaite and Hainey. Then the detective shook his head slowly.

"If it were Unger, now—" he said abruptly, and halted, a curious expression in his brown eyes. "I think I'll go down that shaft where he's sitting, and talk to him there. No, Hainey, you and Braithwaite just come to the top of the shaft. I've got something to say to the man, besides the questions I want to ask him. He may be more tractable if he's in surroundings that are familiar."

"I don't like this a bit," said Hainey to the millionaire a minute later, as Masters stepped to the open shaft, found the ladder, and descended rapidly to the small platform below. Looking down, they could just discern the crouching figure of Peter Unger, seated there like a trap-door spider in its nest. He seemed to be whittling a stick, and paid no attention at all when the detective stepped on to the platform in front of him.

"Oh, I don't think Peter's dangerous," whispered the millionaire. Nevertheless, he got down on his knees, peering over the brink of the shaft.

Vaguely uneasy, they watched Jigger Masters bend a little forward, resting one hand on the cripple's shoulder. Evidently the detective spoke low and earnestly, for Unger's head tilted sidewise—as it had to tilt when he looked up.

Then without warning, it happened! A cavernous growl reverberated. Unger partly rose from his creaky camp chair. One arm wrapped itself around Masters' body, while the other seemed to stab at the detective with a knife, and then get caught by Masters' own arms raised in defense. Both men, struggling, fell over into the foot-deep water.

Shouting execrations at the cripple, Hainey went down the ladder as fast as he could slip the rungs from under his hands and feet. Braithwaite swung down to the cross-bars which held the shoring in position. This way, swinging to the ladder where the cross-bars ceased, he was only a few feet behind the trooper captain. Both newcomers flung themselves upon the struggling men. But Masters had already taken command of the situation. Twisting Peter Unger's chin sidewise with his left hand, he had swung once, twice, with his other fist full on the point of the jaw. Peter Unger slumped unconscious. Panting, Hainey snapped handcuffs on his wrists.

"Thanks!" grinned Masters, getting up and brushing the water from his clothes. "I expected something like that, so he didn't pink me. But Lord! I never dreamed he could be so strong! I'm not exactly a weakling, but he certainly had me worried for a minute!"

"Well," rasped the trooper captain. "I'm sticking the sonofagun in a cell at Riverhead. What charges? Any, besides that assault on you? Is he the one we want for the killings?"

Masters shook his head. "I don't know yet—I doubt it. But hold on to him. I don't think I'll bring any charge of assault. But he ought to be in jail a while—for his own sake."

"For his *own* sake!" echoed Hainey incredulously. "Sa-ay, what in hell did you say to him, anyhow, to make him do that?"

The detective's lips twisted in a grin. "I told him to watch out," he whispered. "Said that if he didn't keep his mouth shut, he might be—*the next victim!*"

5

THE INCREDIBLE ERTZ

LATE THAT SAME evening, Marshall Vandervoort, the assistant whom Masters had assigned to the job of making inquiries around generally in that part of Long Island, called up. It was but a signal. Masters merely took down the telephone number given him, and drove down to the village. There from a pay station he called back. He was risking no chance of anybody at Fernycroft overhearing.

"Listen, Chief," came back young Vandervoort's voice. "I been around all over this section. No strangers much around here—in winter time this end of the Island is dead. But I got a lead from the ferryman at Greenport that may amount to something. You know—the ferry across the Sound. The ferryman says that lately, a number of times, there's a car with a Connecticut license come over, and gone back again. The driver was a young man with a moustache nobody around Greenport knew."

"And the car?" inquired Masters.

"A last year's Cadillac—a victoria model. It always drove straight out of Greenport, heading in the general direction of Fernycroft. But I haven't found anybody—even a state trooper anywhere—that remembers noticing it after that. Of course, we can get 'em to keep a lookout for it after this."

"What about the license—the ferry people must have taken it down when it came across. They generally do," said Masters.

"That's right. They did. And I looked it up. But the car corresponding to that license number in Connecticut ain't a Cadillac at all. It's an old De Soto six, a little bus owned by a Swede named Anderson. He lives in Norfolk, 'way up in the northern end of Litchfield County. He'd have to burn up the road to go and come that distance in one day in a light car like that. Anyhow, it was a Cadillac that crossed on the ferry here, not a De Soto. There's no mixing them buses."

Masters frowned. It might be—probably was—just some young ex-rum runner or gangster coming to see his girl in a stolen car. Yet it was thoroughness in tracking down just such tiny clues that, Masters knew, often broke the hardest case.

"I want you to go back after that Cadillac, Vandervoort," he ordered. "Go find it. Find out all about it and its driver. Wait—" he snapped as Vandervoort started to interrupt— "you oughtn't to have any trouble at all. It's a Cadillac—a victoria, you said? Well, get a list of all the Cadillac salesmen and Cadillac service stations in Connecticut—you can get that easily from the Cadillac Company. If they didn't handle the car themselves, they will know about it. Victorias aren't such a widely distributed model at the moment—there probably won't be over twenty-five Cadillac victorias in the whole state. Of course, you may have to look up the towns just across the Connecticut line in New York, Massachusetts and Rhode Island, too, in case the car came from over the line. But the chances are it didn't. Anyhow, you won't have over thirty-five Cadillac victorias to look up, altogether. And if you're sure it was a last year's model, that narrows it down still more. And now, young fellow, *you find me that car!* And don't come back until you do!"

"Gee, Chief, I—I—" there was a stuttering pause while Masters could just visualize his young assistant's red face, then Vandervoort's voice came back determinedly. "Chief, I'll get that car for you if I have to dig every scrapheap in the country for it!"

THEN WHILE HE was about it, Masters drove to the state trooper headquarters to see Hainey. The trooper captain was in and shook hands warmly with Masters.

"Glad you dropped in, Jigger. I was just about to call you up about Peter Unger. You know we got him cooped up in jail. But we can't keep him much longer unless we bring formal charges of some kind. He's already been released once for lack of evidence on that Holworth case, you know."

"Well, if you have to," said Masters slowly, "make it a charge of assault. I don't bear him any grudge, however. I do believe he's apt to be a bit dangerous to people around— but it's the danger to *him* I'm thinking of."

"Then you *are* serious about that danger. Just what do you mean?"

"Nothing much—except I believe he's safer where he is for the time being. I may be wrong, but I have a hunch that there's something concerned with him and this whole case that is a lot worse than just half-craziness. If Peter Unger were at large now, I firmly believe he'd die—or disappear— within a few days. *He has talked too much.*"

"Talked too much! Why, what's he said?"

"I can't tell you, now—if you don't remember. If I told my theory—and if it got to the press, by accident—I might be in just as much danger. They'd probably have a try for me—and I have the greatest respect for their abilities." He twirled his hat absentmindedly as he turned toward the door. "No, Hainey. You keep Peter Unger safely in jail until this case is finished, or until I say the word. I think you'll be glad of it eventually, if you take my advice."

MEANWHILE AT FERNYCROFT, Braithwaite had been given his chance to start the last lap of the work he had been doing when interrupted by the twin tragedies. A third secretary, undaunted by the fate of his predecessors, had appeared at Fernycroft!

That morning, the very day after the garage catastrophe, a placid, self-assured stranger had presented his card to Carey, the state trooper on guard, and had been allowed to give it to Joe Karnett, the houseman. The card was engraved:

NATHAN ERTZ
Personal Service

Joe Karnett scowled dubiously at the visitor. He saw a severely-clad gentleman perhaps thirty-eight or forty years of age, who wore shell-rimmed spectacles. The man had a brown mustache, and hair of the same shade, rather long.

The luxurious mop of hair was gray at the temples. It was combed straight back from the forehead, dividing at the crown into a back-center part after the Continental fashion.

Joe Karnett grunted. He took the card back into the

laboratory, where Braithwaite, unshaven this day and gaunt of cheek from worry, looked at it without interest. Then he happened to read the line of Spencerian pen-writing below the engraved words. This had been calculated to bring a smile of mild astonishment to his lips. It read:

I have decided to accept you as my employer.

"The hell he has!" snorted Braithwaite. "He's got his nerve, I'd say. All right, I'll see the gentleman in five minutes in the front study, Joe. He flatters me!" The millionaire turned back to his work, grunting.

What followed was amazing enough. The caller came back to the small, front study where Sally Holworth and then George Barnes had done their secretarial work. Braithwaite preferred this as a place into which to usher strangers, as his own private study was littered with blue-prints.

"In view of all that has happened, Mr. Braithwaite," began the amazing newcomer who introduced himself as Ertz, "I feel that I am absolutely necessary to you." He captured the millionaire's hand for a brief, firm handshake. "I am a man of courage, as well as competence. I propose to show you just how I can fill a real want. You have a place for me—a place not only for now, during an emergency, but which I can fill permanently to your satisfaction."

With calm confidence, unbuckling his black brief-case and setting it on the typewriter desk, he took a plain chair and drew it up. "I mean to be your confidential secretary, of course," he said. "Please take your usual place, and make yourself completely at ease." He produced a pencil and notebook from the case. And while Braithwaite, wide-eyed, stared with incredulous eyes, the newcomer opened his notebook ready for use.

"Please dictate anything you choose, no matter how technical, pertaining to any phase of your work."

"H'm-m-m-m," said Braithwaite, studying his man. Then a glint of quizzical amusement appeared in his gray eyes. "My work is hard for a layman to understand. You realize that?"

But the newcomer nodded confidently. "Of that I made quite certain. You have been considerably in the public eye of late, even if the exact nature of your work somehow has escaped the reporters. Please proceed!"

Braithwaite suddenly chuckled. Tucked away in the memory cells of his highly-trained brain were dozens of technical phrases, scores of mathematical formulae that only a scholar or scientist would know. All right, he would call this beggar's bluff, and call it strong!

He nodded, and then solemnly dictated two paragraphs. Each was sensible in itself, and full of meaning to a technical man. The two paragraphs, however, bore no relation to each other.

" 'The normal type of Doric temple was a building raised on a three-story basement, and consisting of one main cella-naos, usually supplemented at one end by an opisthodomos, and preceded at the other end by a pro-naos; the whole being surrounded by a colonnade on all four sides, surmounted by an entablature and crowned at the two short ends by gables.'

"You might make a freehand sketch of that," suggested

Braithwaite dryly. Then he proceeded. "Different subject. New paragraph:

" 'If A is the angle between two faces of a prism, and D the angle of minimum deviation for rays of a definite color—both measurable quantities—the index of refraction of the material of the prism for this color is given by the formula:

$$ n \quad equals \quad \frac{Sin \dfrac{A \text{ plus } D}{2}}{sin \dfrac{A}{2}} $$

"All right. Try those on your Chatterbox—and I'll go shave," grinned Braithwaite, helping himself to a cigarette, and then walking away toward the lavatory.

Nathan Ertz, however, appeared unruffled. Within the minute he had the desk typewriter adjusted, and was rippling out an efficient clatter. Then came a few minutes of work with a clean sheet of paper and a pen. Only a moment or two after Braithwaite returned, expecting shamefaced alibis, the astounding job-applicant laid two finished sheets of paper before the millionaire.

The typed copy was letter-perfect! Not only that, but on the second sheet of paper, drawn closely to scale, was a creditable representation of a Doric temple!

Even that did not conclude the marvels. In parentheses below the other typed paragraph appeared a bit of information regarding the prism formula, one which fairly caused the architect-scientist's eyes to goggle in their sockets.

" 'With color change in various transparent prisms,' "
Braithwaite read aloud, " 'the index of refraction does not
increase regularly. These prisms are said to exhibit anom-
alous dispersion.'

"Holy c-cow!" breathed Braithwaite almost shakily.
"What did you come out here for—to *tutor* me, Mister
Ertz?"

"Not at all," denied Ertz calmly. "I simply wished to
suggest that I shall be able to follow your work with a
dependable intelligence. This will prevent absurd errors. I
wish you to realize that I am qualified as a secretary, and
also as an assistant draftsman, able to handle and read the
blueprints and specifications of your models. Also I expect
to make myself useful in your laboratory, as no doubt you
are busy with the last touches on your proposed skyscraper."

"What? My skyscraper—!" Braithwaite leaped to his
feet, his face pale. "What do you know about my models—
my skyscraper?"

"Not so much," responded the amazing visitor placidly.
"Before coming to apply for an important position, I naturally tried to learn all I could about the probable nature
of my future work. That you were an architect I knew, of
course. But I also found out something about the materials
you have been ordering—modeling clay—glass—casting
molds and dies—and that you had made particular stud-
ies and estimates of the New York *Register* building and
presses. It is the *Register's* $100,000 prize contest for the
best design submitted for its new building, that you are
preparing to enter, is it not?"

Braithwaite looked at him sharply, took a long breath.
That was the confidential information he had given

Masters that first day, about his work—the thing he had
wanted kept secret at all costs.

THE YEAR BEFORE, the circulation manager of the sensa-
tional New York newspaper, the *Register*, had conceived a
great idea for getting publicity and increased circulation.
Not a beauty prize, nor a crossword puzzle or limerick
contest—no mere thousand or two thousand-dollar award.
No. But $100,000 in cash, to be paid for the winning
design for the new skyscraper home which the newspaper
was planning, the contest to be open to all the artists and
architects of the entire world!

But $100,000 is a great deal of money—and an unscru-
pulous man can steal an idea as well as a finished plan.
Braithwaite had believed that he had an original, a revolutionary, design that would have a good chance of winning
the $100,000 prize. However, if this newcomer, this perfect
stranger, knew so much about it—

Then a second thought made him breathe easier. The
contest was scheduled to close in only a couple of days
more, at which time all the finished models, cast in plaster,
had to be registered and placed on exhibit in the Grand
Central Palace exhibition room. It was highly improbable
that within the short remaining space of two days, his own
idea could be stolen, his design copied.

The newcomer appeared to read his thoughts. He smiled
in such a way as to win Braithwaite's approval and confidence in a moment. "I need not say, Mr. Braithwaite,
that your secret will remain inviolate with me, no matter
whether I enter your employ or not. You will find me
perfectly trustworthy. The fact that the contest closes
within a few days prevents the possibility of my appropriat-

ing any of your ideas. On the other hand I have, as you see, especial abilities along the lines you most need right now. During the next few days, in the rush of getting your plans and model finished, I believe—I am sure—you will find me unusually helpful. That is why I came straight to you. Having no respect for formal references—they can always be forged—I brought none. But I brought myself, hoping that you would find that the best possible reference."

Braithwaite slowly smiled. It was a relief, now that he pondered the stranger's words. And Braithwaite needed— had to have—a capable secretary and helper in these last overworked moments.

"I suppose you—er—have a notion regarding the amount of salary you will require?" he asked. "I hope you'll be merciful. Remember, I am only a millionaire, after all!" he grinned one-sidedly.

Nathan Ertz, it seemed, had ideas about that part of it. The ideas were both definite and astonishingly moderate. In a courteous, self-respecting way, he gave his answer, which was so eminently reasonable that Braithwaite accepted the proposition without quibbling. Ten minutes later they were at work in Braithwaite's big work-room, and the millionaire architect was explaining with enthusiasm his almost finished clay model from which the finished plaster casting would later be made.

Braithwaite's plan was for a setback skyscraper of forty stories, surmounted by a tower of twenty stories. The tower was the brand new feature, counted upon by the architect to lift his model above ordinary competition. It was something genuinely new, a tower of mirrors!

"This will make it glitter in the sun, as though shingled

in newly burnished silver!" said Braithwaite, showing his clay model to Ertz. "But more than that, it will light some of the streets below, ending canyon darkness in cities! If future builders follow the plan, the time may come when every street in downtown New York has its full amount of sunlight!"

"Fine!" said Nathan Ertz with unmistakable sincerity. "Think of the people in the ground floor offices of Wall Street, even, having real sunlight. This design is superb. It *should* win!"

"It will—unless the cost of this mirror glass is considered prohibitive!" agreed the happy architect, warming toward his new secretary for his appreciation and enthusiasm. "I've looked into that pretty carefully, though, and I don't believe the extra cost will outweigh the benefit and the striking appearance. I hope not, anyhow."

Thus, as they worked together, getting ready for the molding of the finished white plaster model for exhibition, Ertz learned the inside tale—as far as it had been told—of the Holworth tragedy, and the mystery of George Barnes. And also Braithwaite, who was by no means a hermit by nature, found Ertz a sympathetic and intelligent listener, a man evidently of high culture, although as evidently one who had suffered a deep sorrow which made him shun discussion of his own past.

Two or three little things gave the employer a sort of clue, however. The mention of war service had come up. Ertz immediately had stiffened, admitting in a toneless voice that he had had four years and two months of it. This, with certain Germanic mannerisms which crept out at rare intervals, led Braithwaite to surmise that Ertz once had been a German officer of rank.

The secretary had read all the newspaper accounts of the two deaths at Fernycroft, before coming to apply for his post. Now, learning the little more which Braithwaite himself could tell, he puzzled over the mystery. The explosion especially seemed to interest him.

"It sounds to me just like one of those great 33-centimeter air bombs the Zeppelins used to carry," he said. "The hole left by the explosion would be about the same size, I should say."

"But there were no airplanes or airships heard anywhere overhead at the time of the explosion," argued Braithwaite. "We had thought of that."

"Well, whatever it was—" Nathan Ertz paused, shook his head puzzledly, and blinked behind his horn-rimmed spectacles.

They went back to work.

6

WITHIN PRISON WALLS

JIGGER MASTERS, MEANWHILE, had been doing a little talking about explosives himself. Having checked up a bit on Martin King, the absent Fernycroft butler, and Pierre the cook, and found they had really been where they were supposed to be—the one in Canada and the other in bed—he had given them a clean bill, at least temporarily, and turned to more material facts. He talked it over with Hainey.

"About that explosion—I found out one rather odd thing, anyway, Hainey. I've been investigating a little, and managed to get that crabby janitor, Joe Karnett, to open his mouth a bit. At that I had to use a bottle of Old Taylor to pry it open."

"You would," grinned Hainey. "And what'd he have to say?"

"Well, for one thing, he and the gardener—Peter Unger—had made quite a search around in the garage just a little while before the blow-off happened. You know Peter claimed he had seen somebody flashing a light through the glass in the garage door, and was sure it was some stranger who oughtn't to be there."

"Yes, I heard that. Think he was tellin' the truth—or

maybe just pullin' a stall, for what happened later? A stranger poking around, that nobody knew or could find again, would be a pretty good alibi—if you believed it."

"Yes," agreed Masters, "I thought of that. But Joe Karnett said just about the same thing. And Joe said they took a good look-around in the garage. He said at first that everything was just the same as usual—cars all there and locked, and nothing missing. Then I began to check him up, and asked him if he had noticed anything *new* there."

"I see. You were thinking maybe somebody had planted a bomb in there?"

"That was my idea. But Joe said no; the only thing different—the only thing suspicious, if you want to call it that—was a bottle of distilled water. Or rather an empty bottle that maybe had once held distilled water."

"What of that? Lotsa people keep distilled water for their batteries in their garages."

"Yes, but Joe said *they* never had at Fernycroft. They had always had their batteries serviced at the regular battery service station in the village. And that isn't all. The garage here at Fernycroft isn't heated—they couldn't blast a ditch for the steam pipe through the rock under it. It must get down nearly to zero in the winter time, in that garage. Well, no self-respecting bottle of distilled water is going to stand around all winter in an unheated garage up here without freezing hard and cracking up. Any sensible person would know that. So there would be no sense whatever in having a big bottle of distilled water in the place."

"I get you," said Hainey thoughtfully. "You mean, maybe it was a bottle of something else. 'Soup'—nitroglycerine, maybe, huh? That ain't impossible. Any up-and-comin' peterman c'ud cook himself up a gallon or two out of dynamite, especially this cold weather when it don't have to be handled so delicate. And Gee Whiskers, one gallon of soup would just about blow the can off this end of Long Island!"

"But hold on; there's one thing you haven't considered," said Masters, looking at the trooper captain keenly. "The focus of the explosion, judging from the hole it left, was almost exactly beneath the spot in the garage where the little car that Barnes used usually stood. How would the bottle have got over there from the side shelf where Karnett and Unger saw it? Certainly Barnes wouldn't have lugged any high explosive over there."

"Yeah? Lemme think a minute. Now I got it! Braithwaite told Barnes to put in gas, oil, and alki, didn't he—told him the car hadn't been used much. Well, maybe Barnes was a thorough cuss and, having finished all that, he looks around and sees that bottle. 'Maybe I'd better fill up the battery,' says he. And so he pours the stuff in, thinking, o' course, it was distilled water. And then, if there was the slightest leak or short anywhere in the battery, the minute that stuff hit it—zowie! Barnes goes away from there in a pink fog!"

"Well, you've figured it just about as I did," said Masters, nodding. "Certainly Barnes wouldn't have blown himself up deliberately. Until we have some better explanation, I think yours is as good as any."

It was when he went back to the house at dinner time that Masters met the new secretary for the first time. He looked at him intently, but all he saw was a quiet and rather scholarly looking person such as one would expect doing secretarial work. And Masters had a great many more

important things than male secretaries on his mind just
then.

ALMOST AT THAT very moment, had Masters but known
it, his warning as to the safety of Peter Unger was becoming justified. For just then a young man, well dressed, with
a pocketful of good cigars, descended from the train at
Riverhead and made his way to the jail.

He passed around the smokes generously, and chatted
with the desk sergeant. He was a special writer for the New
York *Register,* he said, showing his press card. News was
slack. He had proposed a double-spread Sunday feature on
the mystery man of the Fernycroft case, Peter Unger, so he
would like a chance to interview the man.

"I might get a hint on this case, from something he'd say.
All of us feel pretty sure that Peter Unger is the real killer,"
he confided. "Now that reward that's been offered—"

He lowered his voice, telling the desk sergeant that he
had a strong hunch he wanted to follow. And if the hunch
worked out, so that Peter Unger could be proved guilty, the
desk sergeant could share in the reward!

That was too tempting bait. The reporter, Mr. Lloyd
Kendall, according to the press card, was allowed to place a
chair just outside the barred door of Unger's cell, and start
in with his line of questions. For a time the sergeant, lack-
ing anything important to do, lingered about and listened.
But it seemed to him that the cripple was divulging absolutely nothing of interest—in fact, refusing to answer at
all, in most cases. So the sergeant finally gravitated back
to his desk, Lloyd Kendall being left to his own devices
with the prisoner.

He had almost finished the interview, it developed.

Rising, he held forth his hand for a shake. Peter Unger scowled, but took it unwillingly. And when the two hands separated, he looked down at a folded bit of paper left in his calloused and dirty palm.

"What's this?" he growled surlily.

The newspaperman stepped close to the bars. *"Befolg Vorschriften!"* ("Obey instructions!") he said in a low, grating voice. Then he changed manner, and bade Peter Unger and, a moment later, the desk sergeant, a cheery good-bye. He promised the sergeant he would be back again in a day or two with some new angles to the case.

And that was the last thing the desk sergeant or anybody else ever saw of him. When a wildly excited telephone inquiry was made a little later, the New York *Register* not only stated that there was no "Lloyd Kendall" there but that there never had been. Anybody by that name showing a *Register* press card and claiming to be a *Register* reporter was an impostor and was to be arrested immediately.

But the Riverhead police had much more important questions to ask "Lloyd Kendall" if found, than any mere details about a faked press card.

For back in the jail cell, after the visitor had gone, Peter Unger had stared at his retreating back with surprise not unmixed with fear. Then he had glowered down at the folded slip, and clumsily opened it, muttering to himself.

It was a typewritten note. Evidently the ribbon was an old one and badly faded, for the characters were almost too faint to read. Peter Unger had to squint his deep-set eyes, and move into the direct rays of the corridor light, in order to decipher it. The message was in German, with no salutation and no signature. It read:

Du hast zu viel in betreff dem Geheimbund gesagt.

Wiederkaust und verschlingst diesen Brief.*

A choked sound came from the throat of the crippled gardener. He got up, as if to call after Lloyd Kendall; but the outside door had slammed. The visitor was out of hearing.

For a full half hour then the prisoner paced up and down his narrow quarters, growling to himself, stopping, and turning his head up and sidewise at each sound from the outside corridor. Plainly he expected something, probably sudden disaster, to come to him from that direction. The crumpled note still was clutched in his sweaty hand.

At length there came the sound of approaching steps. The desk sergeant and a Greek from the nearby restaurant who supplied meals to the infrequent prisoners at the jail, were coming with supper.

Peter Unger crouched back in a corner. His big hand leaped to his mouth. His teeth chewed the paper, and he grimaced. Perfumed stationery. Damned stuff had a sickish taste....

But by the time his evening meal was placed before him, Peter Unger had gulped down the shredded letter. He sat down to eat, though with little appetite.

Midway in the repast, he stopped, laying down his knife and fork with a clatter. A gusty exclamation burst from his lips. He arose to his bent position of walking. One great hand was pressed to his left side. A roaring bellow of pain and terror resounded amid the cramping walls of the jail.

---

* You have talked too much concerning the secret society. Chew up and swallow this letter.

Then, as jailers and policemen came running, Peter Unger fell, all doubled up with that awful cramp in the muscle of his heart. His screams lasted only a single minute. Then they ebbed, and he lay silent, relaxing little by little from that final convulsion.

Peter Unger would blab no more secrets.

7

WHO NEXT?

JIGGER MASTERS WAS one of the first who heard the news. Hainey had telephoned him. But by the time he reached the jail, there was nothing to do but wait for the autopsy.

At the conclusion of that surprising examination, the Medical Examiner for the county signed his official report, looked from the impatient Jigger Masters to the white-covered form on the enamelled slab that had once been Peter Unger, and shook his head dazedly. "What I can't understand is *why!* Why, in the name of God! For, from what we've seen, the man couldn't possibly have lived more than a few months longer at best. About the worst case of *arthritis deformans* I ever saw! Then why hurry him—?"

"It *was* poison, then!" exclaimed Masters, his eyes gleaming.

"It was poison, all right. Five or six of them, in fact! Almost like a toxicologist's cocktail, that coffee he drank—if it was administered in the coffee, which seems likely. A dash of this and a trace of that... all glycosides, though. Now, that's rather peculiar... hm-m."

With an impatient stride Masters crossed the room, looking down at the report.

"Nearly a grain of oleandrine!" he said. "Lord, that's plenty in itself! Oleandrine! Why, Doctor, that stuff's an amateur's poison!"

"Eh? What do you mean by that? It seems to have worked as well as hyoscin, anyhow. Stopped his heart in a hurry."

"I mean— Well, d'you remember that succession of mystery deaths down at Pass Christian, Mississippi, about five years ago? The ones they thought were due to liquor from British Honduras?"

"Seems as though I do recall something about it. All accidental, weren't they?"

"Yes. But damned frightful, just the same. It turned out that all the butcher shops around there bought their wooden skewers for roasts from an old negro who whittled them by hand. The negro was half blind, and innocent of any wrong. He just happened one day to use the wood of oleanders, which grow thickly down there along Bay St. Louis and the bayou back of it. Merely having these extremely poisonous skewers in the meat while it was cooked, killed eight or nine people before the reason and source were discovered!

"Few people know that the common oleander is deadly poison. Most especially the leaves. An amateur can gather a handful—merely go to the florist and buy a potted oleander for fifty cents—stew the leaves a while, and then kill a regiment. The poison has little taste, and a slight odor resembling perfume."

"But I can't see—" hesitated the doctor. "Even if that supposed reporter were a fake—"

"The murderer, without a doubt!" snapped Masters. "He

came here to Riverhead with just one idea, and that was to kill Peter Unger. He didn't go near the restaurant, so it's unlikely he doped the coffee which was brought in later. But it doesn't really matter. He gave Unger *something,* maybe a piece of candy, with oleandrine in it. And it worked! The only thing that puzzles me greatly is that stuff you found in the stomach. I want to look at a bit of it under a microscope. If it really is paper, it must have been a message—and I'd surely like to read it. Find me one of those pulpy pieces, will you, Doctor?"

The Examiner got up and came back in a moment with a sodden bit of whitish fiber on a clean glass slide. Masters accepted it with a nod, and then studied it for some moments under a hand lens.

"I won't need any higher magnification on this," he said quietly. "It's paper, all right—a cheap and porous sort of bond paper. Spongy texture, almost like sleazy cloth. Well, if there ever was anything written on this, it's gone now."

As Masters came out of the county building, a young man was just driving up in a car. He waved at Masters. It was Vandervoort.

Vandervoort was grinning as Masters came up. "Got it, all right—that Cadillac!" he exclaimed triumphantly. "Located it, fake numbers and all. The driver, or whoever it was had been using it, had simply put the right license plates back on, and then shoved the fake ones back up under a beam at the back."

"I didn't think it would be too hard to find," said Masters dryly. "Who's the owner?"

"His name is Isaac Abeles. He lives in a big place at Madison, Connecticut. Hell, he's a millionaire—the last person in the world you'd think would be mixed up in anything like this. But here's the amazing thing—*he's the president of the Upton Flat Powder Company!*"

Masters gave a low whistle. "Now we are getting places! What was his story? How did Abeles explain those false license plates—or did you ask him?"

"Didn't ask him," responded Vandervoort. "Couldn't. He's in Florida—Miami—been there a month or more. Goes down every season with his wife and daughter. There was nobody at the place just then but the gardener and his wife, who are acting caretakers, but I got on the good side of them and they talked quite a bit. They didn't know I was a dick, of course—thought I was an oil-furnace salesman."

"Nobody at all there, huh? House empty?"

"No. Abeles has a male secretary, a cousin by marriage or something to Abeles. It was the secretary that's been driving this Cadillac around, the gardener says. Louis LeNarre—that's the secretary's name—was a bright student at college, but he's quite a gay boy when his boss is away, according to the gardener. Unmarried—spends most of his days and nights in New York. Just runs out here to the Long Island factory once in a while to report on it while Abeles, the big boss, is away."

"You didn't see this LeNarre, you say?"

"No, he wasn't there. But I got a pretty good description of him from the gardener: about twenty-seven, gray-eyed, five feet ten or thereabouts. Good swimmer, pretty strong though not fat, doesn't smoke, chew or drink much. Wears good clothes, and isn't either ugly or good-looking. Just ordinary features— Just about what the ferryman said."

"Uh-huh—and that might be Braithwaite or that cop

there or a couple of million other fellows," said Masters with a snort. "You could arrest half the lawyers and doctors under thirty in the United States with a description like that. Well, it's something, anyway. Tell you what— Suppose you run out to the powder factory and find out what they think about this LeNarre out there. Find out how often he's been around lately, what he did when he was there. And you might make sure nobody saw him strolling carelessly away with a gallon bottle of nitroglycerine under his arm. Though I have an idea they must have to keep a mighty careful check-up on stuff like that."

Masters stopped, lighted a fresh cigarette, and went on. "Then when you get back, do a check-up on Abeles. Find out if he really has been in Miami all along—what his history is—all about him. Now hop to it!"

DRIVING LEISURELY BACK to Fernycroft, Masters pondered on the latest murder—that of Peter Unger—and what might possibly lie behind it all.

"Almost every cunningly devised murder scheme—and there's no doubt there's something deep behind this one—resolves itself into a multiple killing in the end," he reflected. "The killer commits one murder, and then has to keep on committing others. I wonder who is in greatest danger now? If I were writing life insurance, darned if I'd solicit business from this new secretary chap, though—Ertz, is that his name?"

The car rasped on the bluestone drive, as it turned into Fernycroft. Out at the southeast corner, masons were hurriedly rushing up the gray stone walls of a new garage. To accommodate the new machines bought since the explosion, a tent like a sideshow shelter had been erected.

Here Masters saw a Ford, a Nash, and a Chevrolet light truck. One space, that which would be temporary shelter for Braithwaite's new big car, was empty. Masters drove his Studebaker coupé into that flimsy-walled stall.

During the rest of that day the detective was busy getting a further working knowledge of the lay-out at Fernycroft. Braithwaite and Ertz, after brief greetings and giving Masters carte blanche in respect to his needs, had gone directly back to the laboratory. There Masters saw them resume their task of setting glass in the big molds, preparatory to the job of pouring the gleaming white plaster of the show model.

Under the direction of the housekeeper, Martha Karnett, Masters chose for his quarters the small room which had been given to George Barnes. This was convenient to the phone, which had no extension on the second floor, though the house phone system reached most of the rooms.

"You *will* be careful, won't you, Mr. Masters?" Martha Karnett urged, placing a hand on his forearm and looking up at him with serious brown eyes. "I don't know for the life of me what to expect next! Poor Miss Holworth and Mr. Barnes! Sure, they didn't ever do anything to anybody, did they?"

The detective looked after her thoughtfully after she had gone. He had already made up his mind that she was completely innocent of any connection with the affair and, better still, entirely trustworthy in every way. Now Masters ran over in his mind what the housekeeper had told him of the others in the house.

Her husband, Joe, was a good hardworking man, and a good husband. Perhaps a little grouchy the last few years—

but who wouldn't be, after losing all his savings in that big New York bank failure. "It was to've been put into a Connecticut farm for our old age," Martha had explained, shaking her head.

According to Martha, too, both Maudie her daughter, and Lucy Borden, were good girls—boy-crazy, of course, but that was to be expected at that age. Pierre, he was the best cook in the world, except when it came to pie. No foreigner ever could make a half-decent pie, anyway. Martin King, who would be back soon now, was a solid, comfortable fellow, not flossy enough for a fashionable place, but a reliable, competent butler.

Those two poor fellows upstairs, Dr. Spinelli and Mr. Stonewall J. Browne—she very carefully did not call him "Static"—were people who had suffered misfortune. They kept to themselves mostly, and so Martha naturally invested them with virtue. The practiced jokes of the blind man were harmless things, though some of the sounds did make a body's flesh creep.

"And Mr. Ertz, this new secretary?" Masters had casually asked. "You like him?"

"Oh yes indeed!" The housekeeper had been quite enthusiastic. "He's so courteous and nice. A fine man, I think, and so chummy right away with the master. I'm glad Mr. Braithwaite has got somebody good to help him at last. Poor little Miss Holworth was all right, but she didn't know very much, I'm afraid."

THAT EVENING AT dinner, contrary to Masters' expectations, both Braithwaite and Ertz ate with him, though there was no thought of dressing. The millionaire and his helper expected to go right back to the laboratory, and continue their task of setting glass in the molds for the model. They would work until eleven o'clock or midnight. Next day or evening, the plaster of Paris would have to be poured.

Braithwaite was in high spirits. "I know it's wrong of me, after everything that's happened, to feel so cheerful," he admitted. "But I just can't help but feel that I'm going to win. Ten, twelve months I've been working night and day—I've hardly taken time out even to eat and sleep. But now it's almost finished, and it's worth it! I tell you, my model is going to *win!*"

"Here's to deserved success!" toasted Ertz, raising his half-emptied glass of wine, and they all drank enthusiastically.

Masters had been studying the new secretary, finding Ertz a likable fellow indeed. If there was anything mysterious about him, it certainly did not appear. He talked well, though modestly.

Over the dessert and coffee, Masters brought the conversation back to the murders, and in a most unexpected way.

"Just how much do you two men know about a secret society of the Fifteenth Century known as the Rosicrucians?" he asked casually. "Has anyone, for instance, approached you, Mr. Braithwaite, with any exceedingly peculiar proposition—similar to life insurance, perhaps, but having more to it than that?"

"Rosicrucians!" repeated Braithwaite amazedly. The color of enthusiasm slowly drained from his cheeks, and he regarded the detective wide-eyed. "Lord,—where *did* I hear anything like that before! I know now—Peter Unger!

But just what are these Rosicrucians you just mentioned, Masters?"

"Suppose you tell me, first, what Peter Unger said," countered the detective grimly. "And I'll ask, too, that what you have to say goes no further than this room." His keen eyes rested for a moment on Nathan Ertz. The latter bowed solemnly.

Braithwaite considered, frowning. "Why, I—I am just trying to remember," he said in a hesitating voice. "It sounded so crazy, so senseless, that I didn't pay much attention. Peter Unger was always talking wildly. Something about a rosy cross which would crush out tyranny. He had it mixed up with that river which is said to flow under Long Island. I told you something of that, that first day, didn't I?"

Masters nodded. "Tell me again. All you can remember."

"Well, it was a lot of crazy meaningless stuff about 'waters under the earth.' And oh, yes. One time he asked me if I thought *I'd* ever want to disappear! I supposed he'd heard something or other about those threatening and cranky letters I'd received. I just laughed at him. He was serious, though. He told me every rich man had to think of that possibility, and asked me did I really believe Ivar Kreuger, that big Swedish match manufacturer and embezzler, was actually cremated? He claimed that only a wax image of Kreuger was burned; that the real man disappeared, *alive!* In fact, that he just found the load of trouble facing him too intolerable, and arranged to disappear, changing identities, and living thenceforth as someone else, a long way from Sweden!"

"H'm-m-mm. Did he mention any others?"

"Oh, yes. He claimed that Mary, Queen of Scots, never was actually beheaded. Charles the First, the same way. And many others. They just disappeared, according to Peter, their places being taken with wax images. It was all the craziest nonsense, just like that!"

"Wait a minute—I'm not so sure!" said Masters. "You're arguing with history now. The encyclopedias mention an Order of Rosicrucians—founded supposedly in Germany about the Fourteenth Century. At first it was intended primarily as a benevolent and cultural society, and some very big men were supposed to have belonged to it—Baron Rosenkreuz—Francis Bacon—our own Aaron Burr even. There were some very odd popular beliefs about it, one of them—probably instigated by the Italian, Cagliostro—being that it helped people to disappear."

"Helped people to disappear!"

"Exactly. Suppose you, for instance, were Charles I, King of England, waiting in the prison to be beheaded? Or Louis XVI, waiting to be guillotined? You would be mighty glad, wouldn't you, to be able to have someone else substitute for you, and slip out yourself and hide away under another name?"

"But it would be impossible! Those people were actually executed! And you couldn't get anybody to let himself be hanged or beheaded in your place!"

"Why not? People—despondent, half crazy perhaps— have offered to take others' places at executions. Suppose you, for instance, instead of being Charles I, were a poor man, suffering from a fatal, an agonizing disease—like cancer, say. Suppose you had a family in danger of starvation—and someone came to you and offered you a small fortune to take the place of a man about to be executed. Wouldn't you consider it? Slow, painful, certain death on one hand, and your family left to suffer want; a quick, merciful death on the other, and your family left provided for against all privation and want? I certainly think I would be inclined to accept the proposition."

"And your society—it provided the substitutes?"

"That is what Cagliostro and popular belief claimed, arguing that it would be helping the poor. But come down to a more recent time. Suppose you were a big financier—your companies had been mismanaged—perhaps were on the verge of ruin. You were certain to lose your entire fortune, and perhaps go to jail as well. You are crossing the English Channel, say, in an airplane. You step into the washroom—and that is the last seen of you! Supposedly you fell overboard. A man is later found, wearing your clothes, carrying your papers, and with his body smashed beyond recognition by a fall of three thousand feet or more. But it is actually your double, not you! It would take careful cooperation—the most detailed arrangements for you to escape afterward—but you can grant that it would be possible."

"But— But Lowenstein, the great Belgian financier, was supposed to have died that way only a year or two ago!" gasped Braithwaite. "You aren't suggesting—"

"No; there never was any crookedness or other suspicious circumstance proved in his case, I believe. But I was just pointing to possibilities."

Braithwaite gasped. "But you said the Rosicrucians were a benevolent order! Things like this last would be pure crime!"

"I didn't say the Rosicrucians had anything to do with it—either the original order or any similar modern organization that might ever have been planned along the original lines. I was merely taking up that particular tradition of the old order about helping people to disappear. What more plausible than that some brilliant criminal mind—with a deep knowledge of history, of course—should see in it a remarkable opportunity for profit. He could organize a small band, engineer escapes for men like Kreuger—Capone—even the Loeb and Leopold boys. You must admit that any of those almost would have gladly paid a huge sum to escape the punishment of the law and begin life all over again, under a new name, with a share of their original fortunes. And progressing from that—from helping people disappear with their full consent and cooperation—what more logical than the next step of helping them disappear *without* their consent? Kidnapping, in short!"

ERTZ WAS STARING, his eyes fascinated. Braithwaite was gaping. Then he shook his head. "But Peter Unger's crazy signs—his mutterings about 'rosy crosses', and 'water under the earth'—!"

"Supposed to be part of the old Rosicrucian rites. It would be just like the twisted criminal brain that could evolve such a ring to appropriate the rites and pass-words of the real order. Such a burlesque would tickle his twisted sense of humor. You do not for a moment think that any actual, respectable order would tolerate such a half-crazy member as Peter Unger was, do you? Also there is the way he was killed—what more typical of the modern, cold-blooded gangster?"

"But—but what has all that got to do with Fernycroft—with me?" demanded Braithwaite dazedly.

"I don't know—that's what I'm trying to find out." Masters lighted a cigarette. "But we do know that there has been a definite series of murders here. Three, to be exact. That the murders are just coincidental—without any connection whatever, or common purpose—is inconceivable. In any case of multiple murder, there has always been found underneath them all, some definite, fundamental purpose. Until that purpose is achieved, or made forever impossible, any one who gets in the way is apt to be crushed. I am exempting those rare cases of genuine homicidal mania, you understand. This may be one, but I doubt it.

"All right. The three deaths which have occurred here have *not yet* accomplished any definite purpose, analyze them as you will. No one man, conceivably, could have cherished a personal hatred against a poor, half-sick stenographer, an assistant detective, and a crippled miner-gardener who had only a few months to live, even if left to himself. Particularly, when you stop to think that the detective, Barnes, came into the picture very casually, after the murder program had already begun!"

"That is sensible," nodded Ertz. "You mean, he just got in the way?"

"Call it that. But let's go back for a moment. We're presupposing a criminal ring of the sort I've mentioned. What would be the most important objective of such a criminal ring in the vicinity of Fernycroft?"

"You mean *me?*" said Braithwaite, turning white. "My money—?"

"Perhaps. What I've been driving at, however, is the fact that the menace, whatever it is, *still exists*. Right now three murders have been committed. At a guess, one I'm ready to abandon any time new evidence comes to hand to disprove it, Peter Unger was one of the ring planted on you here at Fernycroft. He was to get the lay of the land—make investigations towards future action.

"But Peter was really cracked. He got worse, too, as his illness progressed. So they had to do away with him. Especially when he nearly gave the whole show away with his mad muttering, following Sally Holworth's death."

"But why should they ever kill that poor girl?" cried Braithwaite. "Sally meant nothing to me."

"No, but perhaps she was too close to you and your business. They may have thought her more of a confidential secretary than she actually was. Anyway, they played safe and eliminated her. George Barnes got his for the same reason. And now, Mr. Ertz, have you thought well of the possible chances *you* are taking, acting as secretary to Mr. Braithwaite?"

"Listen," snapped Ertz. "I didn't have any idea about any murder or kidnapping ring, and I still don't believe it! I did think, though, that for some unknown reason, being secretary to Mr. Braithwaite was a job likely to be dangerous. My life has been all too humdrum—since the war, anyhow. I came to secure a good position—but also in the hope that there might be some excitement in the job!"

"H'm-m-mm. I see. And may I ask just what—and where—you were in the war?" asked Masters quietly.

"No, I'm sorry," denied Ertz, his face clouding. "That is part of my history I prefer to keep to myself. It can make no possible difference. I will tell you—"he hesitated, frowning—"that there is a blot on it. If I had been a rich man," and he grimaced sourly, "I might even have used that mythical disappearance ring you speak of! But never mind: I am not wanted by anyone, I can assure you. Quite the reverse!"

"So long as it has no bearing on matters here, I assure you it will not be mentioned," assured Masters. "But now— All too obviously you are in line, Mr. Ertz!"

"Let 'em try!" said the secretary; and Masters grinned inwardly. This fellow was not German at all, regardless of his German name.

"I doubt if any Teuton could have said just that," the detective remarked.

"I was born in America," frowned Ertz. "Have lived here all my life. What did you mean?"

"Oh well, let it pass. Besides you, I suppose I too may expect the killer's attention—before he gets around to working definitely on you, Mr. Braithwaite." Masters swung to face his employer. "Hereafter all three of us must be on the watch-out. So we'll—"

He got no further. Far away, but distinct, came a dreadful mooing sound, ghastly but ridiculous, like the noises of a herd of starving cattle neglected at milking time.

"Hell, don't mind that!" said Braithwaite with an indulgent grin. "That's just Static Browne. But he must be getting lazy; he's pulled that one before. It's what he calls a radio impression of 'Lowing Cows at Sunrise!'"

8

TOWER OF MIRRORS

ACCORDING TO HIS custom when engaged upon this sort of case, Masters obtained a set of blueprints of Fernycroft from Braithwaite, before the latter went with Ertz back to the laboratory. The prints showed the original structure in all its insane weirdness; and then a second set depicted the changes its more sensible second owner had superimposed.

"I'll just make a rough sketch or two of these, and a drawing of the grounds from that large-scale map you have in the study," said Masters. "You two go ahead, and don't mind me."

So for the better part of two hours he busied himself with the pocket sketches, showing the position of buildings on the Fernycroft estate, and the floor plans of the house itself. Then with these completed, he unpacked his bags.

His room was small, for Fernycroft. It had just two windows. From these, in the moonlight, he could discern the piles of stone and lumber which in due course would be the new garage. The garage walls were up now, about five feet.

The small study where George Barnes had typed, opened into the bedroom on one side. On the other side were a

lavatory and a deep clothes closet. The inner wall opened
into the side-to-side corridor of the first floor.

Single bed, chiffonier, reading table holding a dozen
volumes of assorted essays and novels, a rocker and a plain
chair, constituted all the furniture. Masters pulled back the
rug, but the floor was solid and in good condition. He went
around the walls, but found nothing. Then he glanced up—
and remained looking. There were *two* wires, apparently,
coming down to the inverted ceiling light fixture!

Silently, he brought the straight chair over into position,
climbed up, and peered down into the porcelain bowl. Then
he grinned delightedly, and got down. For several minutes
he paced the floor. Then he hauled a suitcase out of the
closet and took two small objects from it.

These were two notebooks, of a sort which might fit into
a vestpocket. One was red and one was black. Both were
new, blank of page. Still smiling, he took the red notebook, and sat down at the table. With a pencil he wrote
rapidly over four pages. The name of Stonewall J. Browne
(Static) appeared at top of the first page, but every entry
that followed the name seemed to be written in a particularly intricate and erratic cipher. There were paragraphs
of such entries.

When his assistant Vandervoort came in some time
later in accordance with previous instructions, that young
gentleman was surprised to be met by a raised forefin-
ger and a portentous wink from Masters, cautioning
him against talking. With gestures Masters pointed out
the dictagraph in the lighting fixture, and Vandervoort
grinned. He nodded, ready to play up.

"Mighty glad you're back, Vandervoort!" said Masters

then. "I think we've got this case pretty nearly washed up. I've got all the evidence summarized in that little red book there on the table—no, the red one, not the black one. But I'm not going to make an arrest tonight. The killer doesn't suspect we're on to him. Might as well wait for morning."

"It's really the one you said, Chief?" asked Vandervoort, the proper amount of wondering respect in his voice.

"Oh, sure. But come on out to the laboratory. We can talk quietly there, while Ertz and Braithwaite are working."

In a way the ruse was childish, yet Masters counted on its very simplicity for success. And success of a kind crowned the effort speedily enough. Making plenty of noise, Vandervoort and Masters went back toward the laboratory; but at the door of the workroom, Vandervoort, on whispered instructions, darted out of the small rear door, around the eastern wing of the building to the garage. Here he took a place behind the five-foot stone wall of the garage, where he could watch the uncurtained windows of Masters' bedroom.

Less than three minutes later, the lights there flashed on. The watching assistant glimpsed what he had expected, and a grunt of satisfaction escaped him. A black-gowned figure, that of the supposedly sightless Static Browne, had entered Masters' room. Pausing for nothing, the figure tiptoed over to the table, picked up some small object, and crept out. The lights were switched off again.

"It was him—and he can see as well as you or me!" said Vandervoort triumphantly, when he rejoined Masters in the laboratory. "Static Browne! Is *he* the killer?"

"I haven't the ghost of an idea!"

"Huh—then you just meant he was the one that planted

that dicky down in the indirect light bowl, eh? Well, what was it he stole from the table? Was there really anything about the murders in that red book?"

"No," grinned Masters grimly. "Not a thing. At least if he can make any sense out of the scramble of words, he's a better man than I am. Because *I* never put any sense in it!"

BRAITHWAITE AND ERTZ paid no attention to them beyond brief nods as they entered. The two were bent over two immense steel molding forms, each of which would hold half of the gleaming white plaster model; these were open and held at waist-height on low supports like saw-horses. No plaster had been poured as yet. In the bottom of the metal shells, and on the sides, were faintly-outlined ridges, shaped as oblongs or squares.

These represented windows and the spaces between windows on the finished skyscraper. The two men in smocks had finished setting ordinary plate glass into the slots for windows, and now were well along with the task of putting in the small mirrors which would complete the finished model. Both men were working eagerly, furiously, though Braithwaite was almost pale with excitement. And no wonder, nearing the completion of a year's endeavor.

No words were spoken. There was only the tap-tap-tap of measured, quick footsteps on the battleship linoleum of the laboratory floor, the slight clicks as pieces of glass settled into their slots.

In a subdued voice Vandervoort told Masters of his trip to the powder factory.

"They don't like visitors much, and detectives less than that," he said. "However, I managed to pry out a little information. The superintendent, name of Pickell, isn't one of young LeNarre's warm admirers. Fact, I reckon maybe there's a little jealousy there. LeNarre's thick with old man Abeles, and has the run of the plant. He sometimes gives orders transmitted through him from Abeles, an' I suppose it doesn't set any too well with Pickell.

"Anyhow, LeNarre's been out there six-seven times since Abeles went to Florida. He's talked with some of the plant men, too, about nitro. But he sure as hell hasn't taken out any dynamite or other explosive. They don't leave any of that lying around loose for the taking.

"I checked close on that. The last nitro they made was in November. They've got about four thousand cases of blasting dynamite in a warehouse, or rather magazine—forty per cent stuff. But that's under lock and key, and guarded. None of it's missing. No, Chief, this guy LeNarre may be the one you want; but he didn't steal any explosive from the company."

"What's the matter with him making some, up there in Connecticut, or maybe in some place out here in this deserted end of Long Island? Anybody who knew the process could do it, I am sure. So that's your next assignment, Vandervoort. Go back up to the Abeles place at Madison, and find out what you can from the gardener. If necessary I'll get you permission to search the house and grounds, though probably you can work it without that. Then if you don't find out anything there, you'd better come back and work this end of the Island."

In Fernycroft that night there was a conspicuous absence of queer electrical or radio noises. After his short stay in the laboratory, Masters resumed his quiet examination of the downstairs, smiling grimly to himself at the thought of

Static Browne working furiously upstairs, trying to work out a code which had never existed.

Trooper Carey, whom Hainey had assigned as guard, and Maudie Karnett had built themselves a blazing fire in the library. Masters saw them sitting conspicuously close together on the oak settle, and he grinned and passed on.

The kitchens were dark. Corresponding to sleeping quarters on the second floor of this wing, however, there was a spacious and quite comfortable living room opening off the main kitchen. Here also a fireplace supplemented the hot water radiators. Mrs. Karnett sat there before the oak logs, rocking placidly back and forth in a broad willow chair. She knitted a violently blue pull-over sweater, using warped wooden needles more than a foot in length.

Joe, her husband, sprawled on a rickety brown chaise longue, smoking a pipe of bulldog shape, and scowling at the ceiling. His black eyes swung sharply and with an unfriendly glint, as the detective entered.

"I suppose you'll be pussy-footing around from now on," he greeted sarcastically. "Can't even let folks alone who have to work for their living." He brought his rawhide-laced boots to the floor with a thump, and waited with hands on his knees.

"I just came to ask you if you knew a young man named Louis LeNarre," said Masters, drawing out a pack of cigarettes, and taking his time about lighting one.

"No, I don't! Why don't you snoop around and ask Braithwaite?" demanded Joe Karnett in a nasty tone.

"I may do that little thing," said Masters amiably. "By the way, Karnett, just what is your grouch at everyone here? I suppose you realize that you make yourself an object of suspicion by your attitude? Captain Hainey was all ready to lock you up and give you a taste of the third degree. And he may do it yet, just on the principle that a man who acts like he hates everybody, might very well go further than that."

"So he wants to lock me up and murder me, just like he murdered Peter, eh?" snarled the surly furnace man. "Well, let him! I ain't got any secrets. I ain't killed anybody— though Lord knows I'd like to, well enough!"

It was the first time the natural enough assumption that the crippled Peter Unger had died under police methods, had come out. Masters hastened to correct the impression, though he doubted Joe Karnett believed him. Embittered by that tragic bank failure and the loss of his savings, the houseman regarded everything in this remnant of capitalistic civilization with savage cynicism.

"He acts too guilty to *be* guilty, though!" was the way Masters phrased it to himself. "Also, he'd take out his grudge on parasites like Browne and Spinelli, or on rich men like Braithwaite. Never on penniless people, like Sally Holworth or Barnes."

Grimly satisfied, Masters left Karnett to his grouch, and climbed the back stairs to the bedroom of Pierre, the cook. AT THE DETECTIVE'S measured knock a sudden commotion sounded within. *"Sacré nom d'un nom!"* came a squeaky, frightened exclamation. Then the sound of bare feet hitting the floor. At the bottom of the door a streak of light told of an electric lamp snapped on.

"May I speak to you a moment, Pierre?" asked Jigger quietly. "This is Masters, the detective."

"Oh, one thousand pardon! I think: maybe you are one of those other queer ones!" responded the chef in his high

voice. He opened the door a cautious six inches, then threw
it wide. Masters saw a small, swarthy, perky-mustached
Frenchman in a red-and-white striped flannel nightgown
that reached exactly to the floor. In his right hand Pierre
held a long kitchen knife, vertically so the point was beside
his right ear. The edge of the long, wide blade glittered
with new honing. It doubtless would slice into a ham—or
a man—as readily as into leaf lard.

Pierre remembered the knife then, and hid it behind
him, bowing as Masters entered. The latter did not sit
down. He spoke warmly of the excellent dinner that night,
and presently Pierre was all smiles, gesturing with the
knife, forgetting again that he held it.

When pinned down to an expression of opinion, Pierre
shrugged. In his mind there was little doubt. Static Browne,
who walked by night and who made the strange noises, he
was without doubt the killer. Who else?

"All others, they have been good to me. They are the nice
people," said Pierre. Even Dr. Spinelli was included.

At that moment there was a sound of shouting below. A
stentorian voice was calling everyone in Fernycroft:

"All hands on deck! Come to the laboratory!"

It was a tired, somewhat dishevelled but rejoicing master
of Fernycroft calling. Braithwaite had reached the end of
his long endeavor, and wished to celebrate the pouring of
the liquid plaster of Paris into the skyscraper molds. The
plaster was all ready mixed in correct proportion, ready in
two immense cans suspended on trucks. All the glass was
set in place inside the steel molds, and the inner shells of
the molds were well greased with mutton fat.

"Finished a little earlier than I'd expected. This gives

me an extra day," Braithwaite said somewhat disjointedly, when Masters and the cook—the latter with a ludicrous chinchilla overcoat thrown over his nightgown—appeared. "Just in case, you know. Sometimes plaster cracks. I'd still have time for another chance."

Joe Karnett and Nathan Ertz appeared, laden with a tray of glasses, and a bucket of cracked ice in which showed the gold foil tops of several bottles. As the black-robed Static Browne shuffled in, followed by Dr. Spinelli who oddly enough was garbed in a dinner jacket and the rest of a spruce outfit, there was a popping of corks and a pouring of the amber wine.

Masters was glad this had occurred. It was his first glimpse of the inhabitants of Fernycroft as a group. Only Lucy Borden and the still vacationing Martin King were absent.

Browne's staring, pale eyes were turned often in the detective's direction. Yet the man, for all the malevolence of that glare, maintained the fiction of his blindness. He allowed Maudie Karnett, half-shrinking from contact with his long, white fingers, to guide his hand to a glass of champagne.

Masters listened to the short speech by Braithwaite, in which the latter told of his own hopes and dreams, to be put in tangible form by the model skyscraper, and thanked all the members of the household for help and inspiration. But the detective was more interested at the moment in studying Dr. Spinelli. The scientist-religionist appeared aloof, somber, as though the proceeding was one he attended almost as a sleepwalker. His dark eyes were narrow, his swarthy face hatchet-sharp, drawn to a fineness which suggested days and nights of incessant work at his microscope and micro-engraving machine.

When the wine was drunk, Braithwaite and Ertz sprang into action. Wheeling the first of the trucks over to one of the two molds, the architect tipped the suspended can, so a thick, creamy liquid flowed out of the broad spout. Little by little this filled up the shell of the mold. The last few quarts were poured slowly and with extreme care, so that at the end a viscous film of the plaster actually arched upward a fraction of an inch above the edge of the mold.

The second shell was filled in like manner. Then Braithwaite straightened, wiping his forehead.

"That is all, folks," he said, expelling a deep breath. "Finish up the wine, if you'd like. I must leave these molds to set partially—putting a damp packing on top of these exposed surfaces after a few minutes, so they will not harden too much. Tomorrow morning early, Mr. Ertz and I put the two halves together, and clamp them tight in a press. Then, by tomorrow night, the model will be ready!"

The one of the group whom Masters would have liked to have drawn into conversation at the moment, was Dr. Spinelli. The Italian, however, as if he had been waiting like a sprinter for the gun, turned on his heel. Without as much as a word of congratulation or good wishes to his host, he vanished in the direction of the staircase.

No one of that whole light-hearted group apparently had any intimation that before daylight, Fernycroft's dark horror would strike again, removing another of their already diminished number.

9

BAD LUCK RUNS IN THREES

IT WAS BRAITHWAITE himself who gave the alarm next morning. He knocked on Masters' chamber door before seven. There was something in that hurried, drumming sound that suggested panic, even before he spoke a word.

"Mr. Masters! Jigger! Can you come?"

The detective was out of bed in a second. Flinging a blue lounging robe over his shoulders, he went to the door which he had locked for the night. As soon as he opened, Braithwaite came pushing in, a single sheet of paper in his hand. The architect was attired in slippers, corduroy trousers, and a high-necked sweatshirt which bore the stains of much laboratory service. His face was ashen.

"Ertz has *gone!*" he said in a hushed, shaking voice. "This note was on his pillow. Bed not slept in at all!"

The letter was brief, sincere, regretful. It read:

> *Dear Mr. Braithwaite:*
>
> *I didn't tell you before, because I did not want to disturb you, just as everything was coming to completion. But I have to go. Something has come up in my private life which necessitates a long absence—perhaps forever. I wish you every success and all happiness. Just hold my things till I send for them.*

Yours ever,

Nathan Ertz.

"Walked out just like that, eh?" questioned Masters, frowning as he swung to the ashen-faced architect. "You really believe he did?"

"Believe nothing!" retorted Braithwaite hoarsely. "He was—*the third secretary!* He—he has been done away with!"

"All right. Tell me while I dress," ordered Masters tersely. He stripped off robe and pajamas, reaching for shirt and shorts.

Braithwaite, however, knew little. He had slept only brokenly, being nervously wrought up over getting the model finished. Before daylight he had taken a shower, and put on some clothes. Then he had gone to Ertz's room, expecting to summon the secretary's help in putting together, clamping and pressing the two filled model molds. According to the program, the plaster model itself would be left inside the molds and press, until taken in for exhibition to the Grand Central Palace building, where most of New York's important exhibitions were held.

"It doesn't make sense, I tell you!" argued the architect. "As far as I can see, Ertz left without taking any baggage at all! Maybe he didn't even take his coat and hat! I forgot to look!"

"Well, we'll see in due course. There's no hurry about just that detail. How about money? Have you paid him recently?"

"Yes—uh—yes, I paid him day before yesterday."

"You did?" asked Masters dryly. "Hadn't worked very long, had he? Did he strike you for an advance?"

"Yes," confessed Braithwaite. "But what of it? He was worth every cent of it, and more."

"H'm-mm. And just how much did you advance him?"

"Five hundred. But what difference does it make? I wanted him for a companion as well as a secretary. I—I have been a lonely fellow since Jessie died, Mr. Masters."

"I am asking," said Masters, "just because we have to know what did happen to him. If he went away from here voluntarily, that is his private business and yours. But if he got tangled up with this criminal ring, for instance—"

"That's it! I'm willing to bet anything that they got him! That we'll find he was forced to write that letter."

"It's his handwriting?"

"Oh, yes. No doubt of that. I have plenty of samples if you want to get them analyzed by an expert. But Nathan had a feeling of proprietorship in this model and the plans. I'd promised him a share of the reward, if we won it. No, Mr. Masters, I can't believe that he would voluntarily have left just now! If he had been afraid of something out of his past, he might have hidden, keeping in touch with me. He could have hidden right here in Fernycroft, with no trouble, as far as that goes. No sir, I'll bet that we find all his clothes, his hat and coat, and everything!"

Masters immediately got in touch with Hainey and his state troopers, and a check-up was started on all public taxis, all the railroad trains, the ferries from Greenport and Port Jefferson, and even the airplanes at the various air-fields. For himself, Masters went directly to Ertz's room in company of Braithwaite. Together, they went over the contents of two clothes closets and a chiffonier. One brown felt hat, a dark brown wool topcoat, and a muffler often worn by the missing man, failed to appear anywhere. They never did show up, even when the search widened, taking in every chamber and even the basements of Fernycroft.

"It is a fair assumption that he went somewhere, and wore those," said Masters with a frown. Like Braithwaite, all his instincts insisted that something more than a mere resignation and disappearance was indicated here. And so it seemed. For in spite of a mounting hum of activity, a search involving town police and troopers, Nathan Ertz remained missing. No trace of any sort was found of him!

AFTER BREAKFAST AND before Captain Hainey and a vanguard of reporters arrived to swarm avidly over the scene of this newest disappearance, Braithwaite drew Masters to one side.

"I know you're going to think me heartless," he almost wailed. "But after all, before we're *sure* something terrible's happened to Ertz, I just simply have to get that model into the press! Otherwise, the plaster will have to be dug out, cleaned off the glass, and the whole thing done over. And I'm short of time as it is!"

"Come on," said Masters curtly, turning back toward the laboratory. "I'll help you. Do we need any more help?"

"Joe's sweeping up there now. We three will be plenty."

Conscious of a return of the nervous exaltation so noticeable in the millionaire's manner the previous night, Masters took his place with Joe Karnett at the end and side of one of the filled molds. Braithwaite took the opposite end, and the janitor stood between them.

"It's easy enough. Just turn this quickly, and place it exactly on top of the other mold," said Braithwaite. "And pray to high heaven that nothing spills. I think the stuff is just about the right consistency, though. When I give the word, lift it, carry it over, then turn it smoothly but swiftly. All right, lift!" They all lifted. The mold with its contents proved heavy, yet the three men handled it carefully and easily. Only when it was in exact place on top of the lower half-mold and the holding clamps at the side locked, however, did anyone breathe freely.

Now all that was necessary was to place the whole thing in the specially prepared hand press. When this was clamped together and the screws twisted down tight, the two halves of the plaster model would be pressed together so tightly that almost no sign of the juncture would remain.

Braithwaite heaved a deep sigh of relief. "Lordy, I'm glad that's done!" he said, wiping his forehead with a dirty handkerchief. "I've sent in the plans to the committee. Tomorrow morning I'll ride in on a truck with this whole affair, unpack at Grand Central, set up the model, and then I'm free—decks clear for anything or everything!"

"From now on you live under guard, Mr. Braithwaite!" said Masters, his mouth set in a grim line. "The decks are also cleared for the murderer, it seems. Three at least, probably four deaths—and all of them leading to yourself, without a shadow of a doubt!"

"Whew! What do you mean by that, exactly?"

"Carry a gun. Be sure of your locks at night. Let no queer people stand around in back of you when there are no other witnesses present. If you want my honest advice, it is to close up Fernycroft, and live in a New York hotel until this matter is settled. Perhaps that won't suit the police for a while, however."

"It doesn't suit me, either!" said the millionaire with

a decisive shake of his head. "I—I wouldn't feel natural anywhere else. And there are a few ideas I got while designing that skyscraper that I want to dabble with."

Masters shook his head. "Well, that's your business. Only I can't let you be killed, or plundered. H'mmm. There's one person connected with this whole affair I really want to see. No, two people. Doctor Reese and his daughter."

The architect frowned. "But I don't understand! Surely, Sylvia has no connection. And her saintly father—my God, if you dragged him into this mess, he'd never let me as much as telephone to Sylvia again!"

Masters refused to argue. According to his way of thinking, the love affair between his employer and the fair Sylvia was a good deal of a wash-out anyhow. The killer, though, might not be aware of this.

Captain Hainey of the State troopers came in then. And with him were three reporters, full of questions about this latest Fernycroft enigma.

"I'm glad to see you boys," Masters said to the reporters. "Your papers can be a big help to us. I'd like to see a general call sent out for any word anywhere of Nathan Ertz, the secretary. He's missing, under what may be exceedingly strange circumstances!"

"Missing!" exclaimed one of the newsmen. "Another murder, do you think, Mister Masters?"

"Too early to say yet. He may not be dead—but I suspect he is. If so, he's the second man to leave the scene of Fernycroft without providing a *corpus delicti!* And consider at the same time that the killer here, whoever he is, used a subtle poison in a third instance, and stabbed a girl without coming near her body, for a fourth coup. If that doesn't suggest murder, what would?"

The grounds were searched as well as could be done, for snow had already begun to fall. Within three hours enough had come down so that anything like traces of a new grave, or blood stains on leaves and shrubbery, would be hidden or completely wiped out.

Meanwhile, signalling one of the reporters, Masters drew him to one side. "I am taking a car, and running over to Easthampton," he said. "Want to come along?"

The reporter, a lantern-jawed youth named Fiske, who had covered the previous deaths, grinned. "Think Ertz eloped with Braithwaite's lady love?" he asked. "Sure, much obliged for the lead. That's what it is, I suppose?"

Masters nodded somberly. He said nothing more until the two, overcoated and gloved, were seated in Masters' Studebaker.

"Braithwaite will not like this," he said then. "But I think it is due Miss Reese and her father, that they be warned. A little of the spotlight won't be a bad thing, either."

"Oh-ho!" said the reporter with a falling intonation. "Trouble coming their way, huh?" He scanned Masters' profile eagerly. This sounded like a swell exclusive story.

THE REVEREND ELBERT Reese and his tall, auburn-haired daughter dwelt in a modest white-painted Colonial cottage, tucked away on an unpaved road some distance from the water, at Easthampton. As Masters and the reporter drew up outside the white picket fence, Miss Reese, clad in rubbers, skirt, mackinaw and gloves, was just engaged in sweeping two inches of snow from the front walk. Except for her hair, snow-powdered and richly colored, she was not strikingly beautiful, Masters saw. Rather a wholesome, vigorous-looking girl, probably not more than twenty. One who looked at the two visitors with calm, appraising blue eyes. Not the buttery, feather-headed sort to be stampeded into marriage with a man just because he was wealthy, thought the detective.

"Miss Reese?" Masters asked. "I am Mr. Masters, in the employ of Mr. Braithwaite, engaged on the Fernycroft case."

She looked at him for several seconds. Then she nodded. "I remember. You are that detective Chester spoke of, some time ago. There was some trouble with Mr. Unger, wasn't there?"

The girl was completely self-possessed. She made no move to invite them inside the cottage; and after one brief glance at the reporter, whose eyes were eagerly fastened on her, she vouchsafed him no more attention.

Masters briefly explained his handling of the case. Then he found himself in difficulties. Miss Sylvia Reese had no intention in the world of discussing herself or Braithwaite with a complete stranger. So Masters had to content himself with delivering a sort of warning he felt uncomfortably certain would be disregarded. He was right. The girl's frosty eyes flashed with a derisive smile.

"You really can't expect me to take that seriously, can you?" she asked with mockery. "I really don't understand you and Mr. Braithwaite, at all. Why I should be considered a part of his troubles now, is a complete mystery. I wrote him a very full explanation a short time ago, and have no intention of repeating it. Hasn't he told you?" She favored Masters with a close, somewhat puzzled scrutiny.

"I understood that he was not to call on you until this mystery of Fernycroft was brought to a satisfactory solution," he replied somewhat stiffly—conscious at the moment, however, that a tingly, queer sensation like a germinating hunch had been born deep inside his brain. Miss Reese had written, evidently a very definite dismissal. When had Braithwaite received this letter?

"Well," she said with a toss of her head, "I have no quarrel with Mr. Braithwaite. He has acted rather peculiarly at times, but I shall be glad enough to see him again sometime—after my marriage!" And as Masters stared, she gave him a quick smile. "For details, if you really did not know that, look at last week's town paper!"

"Humph! Jilted him, huh?" said Fiske as Masters started the car. "T'ain't every day a girl turns down a millionaire. Let's pick up one of these papers and see."

In a small cigar store they obtained a copy of the local paper. Featured therein was the announcement of Miss Sylvia Reese's forthcoming marriage to Lieutenant-Commander Walter Whiting, U.S.N., son of the Gregory Whitings of Brookline, Massachusetts.

"Humph," grumbled Fiske. "Can't make much of a story out of that. Well, there's the Ertz disappearance, anyway—that ought to be good for a column. How you think we oughta play it up—murder, suicide, kidnapping, or what?"

"Why don't you feature the threes angle?" suggested Masters. "Bad luck runs in threes—and we have lots of them here. There were three secretaries. Now all are dead, presumably. There were three private detectives and three guests. One of the guests—for Pete Unger was really a guest rather than a gardener—is dead. Will the next in line for this killer be a guest? If so, will it be Static Browne or Dr. Spinelli?"

"Why not one of you detectives?" queried Fiske disrespectfully. "He's made just as good a start with you fellows, the killer has, as he has with the guests. Me, I'd lock my doors every night before I went to sleep, if it was me—and then I'd sit up all night watching!"

10

STAINS ON STEEL

EARLIER THAT MORNING, Static Browne had felt the need for humor and excitement. For a long time he had been ready to provide a minor mystery for the attention of anyone who happened to play the big victrola, which stood neglected in one corner of the downstairs living room. But for months no one had touched it, and Static Browne himself almost had forgotten the concealed hook-up he had made…

Meanwhile Captain Hainey and his troopers had been finishing the systematic search for the missing Ertz or any sign of him. They had searched not only the buildings, but the grounds at Fernycroft. At the end Hainey told Braithwaite frankly that unless more satisfactory evidence of violence to Nathan Ertz was found, the law could take no further action. "And now where's Masters?" he concluded grumpily.

But Masters, one of the other troopers said, was away— had driven somewhere else with one of the reporters.

Hainey grumbled some more, got a cup of hot coffee from the cook, and tramped around restlessly. "Where's Braithwaite?" he demanded presently of Carey, one of the nearest troopers.

"Gone up to take a shower and change clothes," reported Carey after a few minutes' absence.

Captain Hainey fumbled in his pocket for cigarettes, took a cigar from the humidor on the living room table instead, and sat down in the most comfortable easy chair to smoke. After a few contented puffs he glanced up to see a haggard, dead-white face regarding him from above the second-floor banister of the stair well.

It was only Static Browne. Hainey scowled, and resumed his smoking.

A minute or two later Trooper Carey came wandering in, saw the humidor and likewise helped himself to a cigar. He bit off the end, struck a match and started to light up.

The cigar never was lighted.

For, upstairs, the black-robed individual with the haggard, dead white face, had grinned and chuckled sound-lessly as he saw that the two below were both concentrat-ing on their cigars—and utterly oblivious to the victrola across the room. Two ignorant and superstitious troopers to play a joke on! A chance like that didn't come every day.

Static Browne left the stair well and shuffled back to his own queer workshop of a room. He reached down behind a wall radiator, and lifted up a microphone to which a wire was attached.

As he did so, the Japanese screen which was placed around his single bed in the daytime, swayed a little and almost fell. But Static, setting himself to speak in his most awesome voice, failed to notice.

At that very instant Trooper Carey was just striking a match for a light, "Damn good Havanas, these," he grunted. "Wish I was a millionaire like Braithwaite, and—"

Across in the dark corner of the room where the cabinet talking machine stood, suddenly sounded a dreadful, pain-wracked groan! It was a deep bass, slow-throbbing, quivering as with terrific agony.

"Cripes!" yelled Carey, leaping a yard backward, and dropping both cigar and match on the floor. Across from him Captain Hainey grabbed for his automatic, staring. Then, looking at the victrola cabinet, he suddenly let out an oath.

"It's just radio, damn it! It's that damned monkey upstairs again—"

"Naw, that isn't a radio! Just a plain victrola—"

But the blood-chilling broadcast planned by Static Browne came now in a suddenly different key. A piercing scream, far different from the carefully-modulated sound meant for the microphone, crashed and tore through the sensitive instrument! Upstairs as well as down, that scream, saw-edged, then throttling horribly into a gurgle, caused hearers to leap to their feet, gasping.

Again! The scream was less in broadcast volume now. There was a terrible bubbling sound, a thumping crash....

In his final appearance before the microphone, though he would never know it, Static Browne had achieved his masterpiece of auditory horror.

JUST GETTING OUT of the Studebaker, Jigger Masters and Fiske heard the screams through an open upstairs window. The detective gave an inarticulate cry, and led the way indoors, his long legs taking the steps three at a time. Fiske followed, his eyes bulging. The reporter had not been prepared for such noises by even one of the milder practical jokes of Static Browne.

In the hall upstairs, a greenish-white Dr. Spinelli backed out after one look into the workshop of his fellow guest.

"*Stabbed! Dead!*" he screeched, cowering, shrinking away from the troopers as they came. Carey caught his arm.

From a door further down the hall Braithwaite came dashing forth. He was dripping wet from his shower, and had a towel clutched around his middle.

"What's this?" he cried. "Some more of that damned nonsense of Browne's? I thought it sounded worse...."

Joe Karnett, in overalls and carrying a shovel, came from the back. Just behind him was Pierre the cook, holding his broad-bladed knife. Still further behind, Lucy Borden, Maudie Karnett and her mother huddled, not daring to approach nearer.

Masters, Hainey and the pop-eyed Fiske entered the cluttered up workshop bedroom of Static Browne. There the black-robed figure lay doubled up, half-sitting, propped against the aluminum-painted radiator. The narrow, bald head was slumped forward against the bony knees. And a red cascade had geysered from his neck, drenching his robe and splashing the radiator, before it gathered in a faintly steaming puddle on the hardwood floor.

"Dead. Stabbed twice in the neck—from the rear," said Masters tersely. "No sign of the weapon, unless it's under him." He straightened from the brief examination, face tense and brown eyes hawklike. "Put everybody in one of the other rooms, under guard, Hainey."

Braithwaite at that instant seemed to come to the realization that he was unclad except for the towel. He had been standing in the open doorway, gazing with horror-

filled eyes down at the dead man and the nickeled microphone lying at his side.

"Gosh, I'd better get dressed," the architect mumbled.
"One of you—Carey, maybe?—want to come back with
me? I'm sort of scared to go into any of these rooms now."

In this wise the place was cleared, until only Masters,
Hainey and the dead man remained in the chamber.

"Better get the photographers and the medical examiner
right away," Masters suggested. Hainey, no doubt from the
suddenness of the shock, seemed numbed mentally and
physically. He moved vaguely in the direction of the house
phone, but Masters called him up short.

"No outside wire up here. Have to go downstairs," he
said. "That way. Hurry it up. I'm going to go over the rest of
the room while we're waiting." He had to shove the captain
toward the stairs. But once started down, Hainey seemed
to regain control of his disordered faculties.

SWIFTLY THEN, MASTERS began a close scrutiny of the
strange room in which Static Browne had spent most of
his sleeping and waking hours. It looked more like a property room than living quarters for anyone. A chifforobe, a
steamer trunk, a rug, two chairs, and the single bed with
a Japanese screen hiding it from the spot where Browne's
body had been discovered, were all the ordinary furnishings.

On a sector on the north wall was built in a radio send-
ing apparatus, its complicated arrangement of switches,
wires, transformers and other parts in metal housings looking formidable to any ordinary eye. Two excellent radio
receiving sets were side by side near the sender. And the
entire wall opposite, save for the three windows looking

out on a roof of curved tiles colored green, was given over
to drums, traps, saxophones, various wind instruments of
bizarre as well as recognized shapes, and then the marvel-
lous collection of noise-makers the dead man had used
for concocting his radio sound effects. Coffee-grinders,
cigar-boxes half filled with dry bones, whistles, reed horns,
oddshaped bottles, sleigh bells, a xylophone, all the violin
family from a squeaky little half-size violin up to a big,
full-sized bull-fiddle.

For the time being Masters disregarded this collection
save for one comprehensive glance. He got down on his
knees, looking at the microphone fallen from the victim's
hand, but not moving it. He followed the wire to the hole
in the floor where it disappeared.

Back over every inch of the bare floor, then making a
close survey of the rug, Masters covered the room as carefully as he could without subjecting it to a microscopic
examination.

Careful not to touch the screen, the detective looked at
it closely. There were faint smudges in a number of places
along the frame. Fingerprints—but probably those of the
dead man himself.

The single bed, covered with two gray Army blankets,
and neatly made, showed a slight depression near the
outside edge. Someone had sat there, but it well might
have been Browne. If the killer had waited there, he had
left no sign of his identity.

One window of the three looking out upon the curved,
freakish tiled roof, was open six inches. It was held in that
position by a patent catch at the side, however, and could
not be opened further from outside. The detective looked

long and carefully at the roof. At this precise spot the snow had been blown from the smooth tiles, destroying any chance of finding incriminating footprints.

Holding open the patent window catch, Masters raised the sash and climbed out to the tiles. Here the roof formed a sort of open porch above the porte-cochère of the main motor drive below. In one queer sweep, however, the tiles slanted up between the windows of Browne's room and the gable of the next set of windows. Without difficulty the detective made his way across this short slant, and found himself peering into a wide open window. This open window gave into the room of Dr. Spinelli!

"Hot-blooded sonofagun, to keep it open daytimes," grunted Masters, sliding one leg through and then climbing to the floor. He stood, surveying the chamber.

In contrast with the clutter of Browne's room, this showed an almost monastic severity. Bed, chiffonier, two straight chairs, a grass rug on the floor, and a small square table holding a neat pile of books, were almost all the furnishings. Beside these, however, was a broad, wide desk with a glass top set on a blotter. The desk was golden oak, and had a swivel chair to match.

On the desk was a slanting book support, now holding a large-print Bible, which was open at the sixteenth chapter of Exodus.

Suspended above the desk was the frame and pantagraph arm of a McEwen micro-writer—or possibly an adaptation of that instrument. The sheet held on the desk, in a frame, showed Dr. Spinelli's clear, slanting chirography:

*6. And Moses and Aaron said unto all the children of Israel: At
even, then, ye shall know that the LORD hath brought you out
from the land of Eg—*

"Stopped in the middle of a word!" reflected Masters. "Could that be when the scream sounded?"

He glanced rapidly at the mechanism of the micro-writer. Dr. Spinelli merely had to write in his ordinary, painstaking hand on the sheet of paper there on the desk frame. These movements were transmitted through the pantagraph arm to a delicate reducing mechanism. The actual engraving on glass was done by a diamond chip, up there in the box housing three feet above the desk. These ordinary characters were reduced so much that a 400-power magnification was necessary before they could be read at all by the human eye.

These details were momentarily forgotten, though, in the thrill of a discovery. In turning about, Masters glanced searchingly across at the white-spread single bed. From this angle he saw the fresh, unwrinkled spread all the way to the floor. And just a fraction of an inch above the floor there showed a small red mark!

Lips compressing to a line, Masters strode across the rug, knelt, and stared at the mark. Then with infinite care he lifted the edge of the linen spread, looking under the bed. Shoved back close to the wall, but clearly visible, was a long-bladed, slender knife with a heavy handle wound with copper wire. And the blade was stained with fresh blood!

WITHOUT DISTURBING ANYTHING, Masters opened the door to the corridor, and waited there silently until Hainey came up from phoning. Then he silently beckoned the captain, and showed him the interesting exhibit.

"Better not touch it until the fingerprint men have a chance," cautioned the detective. "I don't think there will be any marks; our murderer is far too clever a man for that."

"Yeah," agreed Hainey. "But what is that loop of cord? That fishline thing on top of the handle?"

"That ought to explain a whole lot," answered the detective. "There is a loop—right here—at the end of the fishline. Do you get it? That loop fits around the butt of the handle of this throwing knife. And that's the way Sally Holworth was killed without any tracks showing close around her. The murderer threw the knife from behind those cedars, yards away. Then he jerked the knife out and back to him with this strong line. Only the knife flew back and hit that cedar limb, leaving those bloodstains that we found."

"But this fellow Browne—you said he was stabbed *twice!* That couldn't be done with a thrown knife—not the way this stabbing was done!"

"No." Masters considered, twisting one side of his wide mouth. "That means a slight revision of the first guess. Good thinking, Hainey. Probably the killer got to close quarters—behind the screen, perhaps, and didn't need to throw the knife. Just used it in the ordinary way.

"Then just hustled back here and slung it under the bed, without even wiping it, huh?" Hainey sounded incredulous. "If he was too much in a hurry to take off the blood, we sure ought to get a nice set of prints."

Masters shook his head. "There is almost no surface for prints to register. And you know you have to have smooth or slick surface for fingerprints," he pointed out. "You see that handle has rows of copper wire winding. Nothing will show against that. Anyhow, our man—or gang of men—has brains. Finding this weapon under Spinelli's bed is the very best reason I can imagine right now for thinking the doctor innocent!"

"Humph!" Hainey was unimpressed. "They all make slips one time or another," he grunted.

"Mr. Masters! Oh, Mr. Masters, phone call!"

It was the gruff, resentful voice of a reporter, one of the two who had come with Fiske, but who had just now come back from Riverhead to find themselves excluded from something they suspected was a dramatic break in the news at Fernycroft. Hainey's troopers had them sitting together downstairs. One of them had taken the phone call, and tried to wheedle out of the voice at the other end of the line just what the message for the detective might be.

It was Masters' assistant, Marshall Vandervoort, calling from the village nearby, and he was not to be wheedled. He waited until he was certain that his superior was on the other end of the wire, and then his news came with a rush.

"That Abeles secretary, Louis LeNarre, has *disappeared!* He should have been down to the plant yesterday, but did not come. And he has not even written Abeles for two weeks! Abeles is sore, and has been wiring all around New York and Connecticut. But so far no trace has been found of LeNarre since he last left Connecticut. But that ain't all! I got some more news—interesting stuff I picked up right on the Island here."

"Then hop up here and spill it," ordered Masters tersely. "There's been plenty happening here, too. Your man LeNarre isn't the only man who has disappeared—and permanently, probably. Ertz, Braithwaite's latest secretary, has disappeared—it seems to be open season on secretaries. And Static Browne here has just been put out of the way with a knife. So come running!"

THE MEDICAL EXAMINER, accompanied by a photographer and two fingerprint men, had arrived at Fernycroft by the time Masters had finished talking. Hainey called to them from the stairway, telling them to come straight upstairs. Masters himself did not follow. He knew that these men worked better and more thoroughly when not hampered by outsiders.

There was a sound of another car out on the bluestone drive. Masters glanced out of the window, to see Vandervoort, alighting from a taxicab, counting out a bill and silver for the driver.

Masters went quickly to meet him, so that he could talk out of hearing of the reporters. "Now what's that news you picked up on the Island here?" he inquired quickly.

"Well, it's this—*it was undoubtedly your missing boy-friend LeNarre who made the soup!*"

Masters gave an exclamation. "It was! You're sure of that? Where did you find it out—in Connecticut? At the place in Madison?"

"Didn't go there! Used the old bean!" grinned Vandervoort. "I said to myself, why should anybody cart a gallon of high explosive all the way from Madison? Answer, no reason. So I just went to all the renting agents around here in Greenport, Sag Harbor and Riverhead, looking for someone who'd rented a summer cottage in winter. And

I found one, right over on the water, not far from a flag station called Peconic!

"I won't bother you with how I got in. I did. And I found where some suspicious cooking was done on an oilstove, with an old bathtub used as a cooling vat.

"The bathtub, the oilstove, and a carboy smelling of strong nitric acid, had been left. No other signs. But the big and juicy point for us, Chief, lies in what I got out of the rentin' agent. The fellow who rented the cottage paid $75 for three winter months, cash in advance. He gave one reference, sayin' his own name was Oscar Neimeth. The reference was to Louis LeNarre, The Ashes, Madison, Connecticut!"

"Check!" agreed Masters with a nod of congratulation. "Went back and wrote himself a reference, eh? That's excellent work, Vandervoort."

"Fits, does it?"

The detective hesitated. "I've got more than a glimmer now, I think," he admitted. "There's something deep and horrible behind this business, and it's nothing as simple as extortion of money from a millionaire—as I suspected at first."

"Woman mixed up in it somewhere? Braithwaite's girl, I mean."

"He doesn't seem to have one—and that's something I'd just as soon you didn't mention to anyone, Vandervoort. What you and I are going to let out, though—with an appearance of confidential secrecy—is that I have become convinced of Dr. Spinelli's guilt. Hainey is sure to arrest him now, anyway, after finding that bloody dagger under his bed. We'll let the majesty of the law move as far as it wants to go in that direction—just making sure this time that no poison gets to Spinelli in his cell."

"What?" cried Vandervoort, really surprised. "That means you think whoever's doing it has got Spinelli ticketed, too, and all ready to ship to hell for the next trip, huh?"

"Yes, if the State of New York won't kindly help out by electrocuting Spinelli!" said Masters grimly. "This nightmare of murders seems to be moving in sets of three. First, three private secretaries. Then two guests—with a bloody knife left to raise a presumption of murderous guilt against the remaining guest, Dr. Spinelli.

"After he is taken care of, there will be just you and me left to work on!"

"Well, I kind of figure we'll give 'em their hands full first, eh, Chief?"

"Perhaps," agreed Masters, hazelnuts of muscle showing along the line of his jaw. "Anyhow, we stay at Fernycroft. From now on, Vandervoort, you are to stick right with Braithwaite. Sleep in his room with him, if he'll allow that. Accompany him when he goes in town tomorrow with the model. Do you understand?"

"Chief," said Vandervoort with a grin, "I'll stick so darned close to him we'll be tying each other's ties by mistake!"

11

INTERROGATION

THE NEXT FEW hours were hectic ones for everyone concerned.

The district attorney for Suffolk County, Leslie Blodgett, arrived on the scene and insisted on taking charge of the case personally. He was a disagreeable man, one who seemed to resent having to perform the duties of his office. Captain Hainey hated him. So did the deputy sheriff. Masters shrugged, and kept out of the way. Beyond making a clear statement of all he had discovered—and nothing he deduced from the facts—Masters was willing to pursue his own investigation and allow the district attorney to go his own bent.

Of course Dr. Spinelli was arrested at once. Then Blodgett exercised his authority to strengthen the case against the Italian. Masters made no objection, though, he told Hainey there was little possibility that Spinelli could have committed all the murders.

"Unless we are prepared to accept two or more criminals, we will have to exonerate Spinelli. While there may be a gang," said the detective, "I feel sure that all the actual killing has been done by one man. There is the touch of the artist in all of them—and no gang ever is artistic."

After which Masters hunted out Braithwaite and Vandervoort.

"Keep out of the D.A.'s sight," Masters warned his subordinate. "There's no telling what he'll have you doing. And I want you to stick right with Braithwaite."

"Is that necessary now?" frowned the architect. "I really think, in spite of all Blodgett's stewing and fussing, he probably has got a case against Dr. Spinelli. And if so, why do I need a bodyguard? You don't expect to find another killer, do you?"

"No. One will do me well enough," said the detective with a tinge of grimness in his voice. "But the case is deplorably weak. Unless and until we can strengthen it, we have to assume the possibility of being wrong, as far as Dr. Spinelli is concerned. And that means another person than he committed the crimes."

Braithwaite pursed his lips. "Oh, well," he shrugged. "I suppose it will be safer for me. Will you come in with me in the morning, Mr. Vandervoort? If so, you can help me set up the model at the Grand Central Palace. That'll be ticklish business."

"Yes, he'll go," said Masters. "By the way, I'm just checking up on curious points. D'you keep clothes both upstairs and downstairs, Mr. Braithwaite? I understood you had your bath and rooms and wardrobes down here on the first floor."

"Oh sure," chuckled the architect, with a knowing wink. "I can see just what you're getting at. I've wondered why nobody thought I acted suspiciously. That second shower I took, you mean?"

Masters nodded shortly. "According to what you told

me, you bathed before dawn. Then in four or five hours more we find you in a shower again, and this time *up*stairs!"

Braithwaite seemed to find the point amusing. "I have to confess, this business of actually finishing up the plans and model got me worked up plenty!" he laughed. "When I got through with tipping that mold containing half of the plaster, I felt weak in the knees and dripping wet with perspiration! Just excitement and tension, of course. I wanted to relax then, though. So I took a good hot soaking, intending to don this very suit I have on now. It was up in the cedar-lined closet of the room across the hall from Spinelli's. And I always kept some haberdashery there, too. Sometimes, when women guests were here, it was easier to give them my downstairs room, rather than move Spinelli and Browne. Those two would frighten any woman out of her wits, if they took it into their heads to go roaming around nights."

Masters nodded, palpably relieved. "I'm glad for your sake that's the way of it," he said earnestly. "This man Blodgett, to whom I've not mentioned that little point, might consider you a suspect, if he heard. Of course *he* is not hired to exonerate you in any way!

"And, oh yes—when you see that Miss Reese of yours again, I'd warn her to be on her guard a little. There's no telling for sure that the killers won't bother her even yet."

"H'm-m-m." Braithwaite frowned. "I—I have my doubts that Sylvia really is any too anxious to have me cleared and resume calling. She seems so distant in her notes to me. I—well, I suppose I'll get over it. One does."

"Not a case of someone beating your time, is it?" asked Masters jestingly. "You're quite eligible, you know."

"I don't think so. No-o, I hardly believe it. More likely just a case where the old adage about absence making hearts fonder, got into reverse instead of second speed. Like a pig-headed driver of an old-fashioned Buick, trying the standard shift, maybe." He shook his head.

AT THAT MOMENT Hainey, his face eloquent of bitter rage, came striding in. He had managed to get excused from the session before Blodgett, for a few minutes.

"Have you got something to drink—something strong?" he demanded of Braithwaite. "I'm just about to commit one nice, juicy murder my own self, and I need a bracer!"

The millionaire grinned, and went to a cabinet, bringing out a glass-lined silver flagonette, and a small glass. "Here's some. Frere Diacre anisette. Strong enough," he said, pouring the one-ounce portion with a steady hand, and offering it to the captain.

Hainey looked dubiously at the small size of the glass, but with a grunt in lieu of a *prosit,* tossed it into the back of his throat. Then for an instant as he swallowed, his eyes bulged. But he made no comment. It was noticeable, though, that his second glass went down more cautiously.

"Hrrphh! Pardon me, gentlemen!" A new voice, following an apologetic clearing of the throat, interrupted. "I wish to ask if luncheon should be served as usual?"

All four men swung about. A butler stood in the doorway, half-smiling in deference to this being his first appearance since his return from Canada, but otherwise correct. Masters knew at a glance this must be the Martin King who had been vacationing since before the first trouble at Fernycroft Towers.

"Why hullo, Martin!" exclaimed Braithwaite cordially.

"Didn't know you were back! Have a good time? Yes? Well, I suppose you've heard how everything is upside down and crosswise here. A light lunch, with perhaps some cool beer, is the most we can expect, I'm sure, with the district attorney questioning all of us."

Braithwaite looked at his watch. "Why, it's two-thirty already!" he said in surprise. "And I suppose everyone is starved. Why yes, Martin, go ahead and bring in whatever there is. Sandwiches and beer would go well, I think. But if anything else is ready, so much the better.

"By the way, Martin, this is Mr. Masters, and this Mr. Vandervoort—two detectives who are helping me try to get some sense out of all that has been happening at Ferny-croft. If they question you, tell them anything they ask. We have no secrets, now the model is finished and the plans sent in."

Masters looked with interest at this servant, who had been fortunate enough to miss most of the trouble. Martin King appeared to be something less than the perfectly-trained English servant. Rather the independence of the Canadian showed through. And he was not stiff of artificial. The detective fancied that from the first he looked at Braithwaite strangely, though that might well be the effect of coming back to find his well-ordered household so upset. Two or three times the butler's eyes narrowed, and when the orders were given, he swung about with the hint of a frown on his forehead.

Beer, a salad, cold cuts, steaming frankfurters with sauerkraut, and sandwiches were put on the table. King went in to inform Blodgett that these things were ready. And a few moments after that Masters got an opportunity to speak to the butler off at one side of the room.

"I'll want to talk to you later, Martin," said Masters. "But just one thing now. I suppose this is terrible enough to you—hearing that there have been so many deaths. However, when you came in the room there first, I thought that something puzzled you. What was it?"

The butler shifted his weight. "Why, sir," he hesitated. "The master—he is quite changed by all this, I should say. No wonder, of course. He—he didn't shake hands!"

"He would do that usually?"

Martin King colored a trifle. "Yes, he used to. He isn't so formal as lots of folks. That's why I don't mind working for him. He never used to call me Martin. Always 'Rex'! I like that better, too, somehow."

From that moment on, until he left later to go for a little talk with Hainey, Masters walked about Fernycroft like a man in a nightmare.

He thought he knew the murderer at Fernycroft. But the incredible, the preposterous part, was that the man he suspected *was already dead!*

12

LIVE MEN IN A HEARSE

EARLY THE FOLLOWING morning Braithwaite accepted delivery on a big new automobile, the Lancia he had ordered. As soon as the salesman disappeared with his check, the millionaire had Joe Karnett help him fold back the convertible top, and measure the interior space with a carpenter's rule.

Big as the gleaming new car appeared, it did not seem to measure up to the millionaire's requirements of the moment. He shook his head and frowned. A moment later he went inside Fernycroft, and busied himself with the phone.

Masters was waiting. To give himself the appearance of occupation, he lent himself to Blodgett, who was fussing around Fernycroft with plans of the place. Just what bearing such a discovery might have upon even his own theories of the crimes did not readily appear, but Leslie Blodgett was looking for secret passages, hidden rooms which might have been used by the arch-fiend, Dr. Spinelli.

The detective was rather glad of this investigation. Probably some queer things would come to light. Anders Krehbiel, the original designer of Fernycroft, had been an out-and-out madman. When questioned about the architectural secrets of the place, Braithwaite only shrugged. His own adaptations of the original plans had all been in the nature of pulling out partitions to make rooms larger, the levelling of queer slanting corridors, and taking out flights of steps between rooms of the same floor. He knew of nothing more than showed in the blueprints, and did not care especially.

A half-hour later Vandervoort came and touched Masters on the shoulder.

"Will you come out and give us a hand, Chief?" he asked. "Braithwaite and Joe and I and you—we ought to be able to lift that skyscraper, don't you think? And say—" his voice hushed—"Braithwaite and I are going to ride down with the thing, and get a couple of porters to help us lug it into the Grand Central and set it up. But did you see what we're going to New York in? *Did* you?"

"No." Masters turned, dusting his hands. "What is it?"

"A *hearse!*" said Vandervoort, grinning—yet with an uneasy light in his blue eyes. "If you ask me, I'd call that one hell of a thing to carry an entry in a hundred thousand dollar prize contest! But this egg Braithwaite has his own ideas. He says he can't allow the model to be joggled any. And so I get a free ride in a graveyard delivery—a little bit ahead of time."

"H'm-mm." Masters began to frown, but his eyes held a calculating, cornered light. "Just one piece of advice then, Vandervoort," he said gravely, dropping a hand upon his assistant's shoulder. "Don't eat or drink *anything*—or accept any smokes—from anybody while you're gone! Will you do just that?"

Vandervoort started. "Well, I'm no dumbbell," he said

slowly. "I sure as hell won't. But tell me, Chief, you aren't picking *Braithwaite!*"

"No, I'm not picking Braithwaite," answered the detective in a thin voice. "However possible it might be for a man in his position to get an insane hatred of secretaries, and turn murderer, I don't think that. No, it's just a precaution, Vandervoort. I have the strong feeling that you and I are going to be bad life insurance risks from now on!"

"I see. And you don't exactly like this trip in the hearse? Think it looks too—too—" Vandervoort could not find the word he wanted.

"Apt? Yes, in a way. Perhaps unconsciously apt, which would make it just that much more horrible! But let's get this model out into the hearse. I suppose Braithwaite is waiting—"

The molds, even when taken out of the hand-press, proved too heavy, with their load of plaster and glass. Carey and one other trooper had to be requisitioned in order to carry the load out to the waiting hearse without danger of dropping it. With Joe Karnett, the two detectives, and the architect himself, they succeeded then.

"Lord," breathed Braithwaite, mopping his brow with a handkerchief in spite of the chilly air, "now it's that far, anyhow! I'll be ten years younger when the thing is actually up on display! Now, driver, I want you to take the bumps slowly and carefully. After you get on the concrete, there won't be much danger. But I'll give you a liberal tip for extra care just the same."

"Right you are," said the man respectfully. In spite of his knowledge that this was a mere commercial burden, he had a grave, funereal air which probably was natural to his place behind the wheel of the hearse. Vandervoort grimaced back at Masters as the big car slowly gathered speed. The detective waved, and turned back into Fernycroft.

Here, as soon as he made sure that Blodgett, Hainey and their helpers would be engaged in the third-floor attic and the corner towers for some time to come, the detective made his way rapidly to the studio-laboratory in the rear of the building. An hour of undisturbed investigation here was something he had wanted for a long time.

The two-story wing was semi-detached from the rest of Fernycroft, being connected by a short passage. Except perhaps at summer noon-day, the main part of the house, three-storied and with towers of various sizes set erratically here and there, excluded all except north light from the laboratory.

The walls were rough plaster, neutral tinted. There had been no attempt made to make it seem anything other than the workroom of a man who dabbled some in the optical branches of physics, but whose main interest was artistic creation.

The original clay model of the skyscraper stood neglected there in one corner. Its glass had been removed, and in drying it had cracked in a number of places. No doubt Braithwaite would consign it to the scrap heap, as soon as he thought of it.

The two oversize milk cans which had contained the liquid plaster, still were slung on their truck supports. They had not been cleaned, even. The low sawhorses lay just as they had been kicked aside.

SLOWLY AND THOROUGHLY Jigger Masters went over the room, his footsteps resounding hollowly from the five walls. Much of the apparatus explained itself readily enough in terms of Braithwaite's experiments with light. There were diffusion mirrors of many shapes and sizes, so that anyone walking about caught weird glimpses of himself, as in a Coney Island Hooligan Castle. Sometimes he was fat, sometimes tall and attenuated. But Masters got no smiles from these reflections.

A clutter of lumber for scaffoldings, and several small step-ladders lying on their sides, made up a pile along one part of the north wall below the large windows. Behind these, poking along as he pulled a ladder out of the way, the detective pounced upon a pair of objects, seemingly tossed there as carelessly as all these other articles.

These were an empty sack which once had held a hundred pounds of unslaked lime, and a one-gallon glass carboy. The latter bore no label; but when Masters lifted it to his nose there was the unmistakable acrid smell of fuming nitric acid!

"Empty! And that one Vandervoort found in the cottage at Peconic—*it* was empty, too!" said Masters to himself. Lips compressing in a grim line, he corked the carboy with its chained glass stopper, then wrapped it in the sack.

Putting this to one side for the time being, he turned his attention to a pair of large metal sinks, like laundry tubs, on the east wall. These two, and a small sink for the washing of hands, stood side by side, all supplied from the same hot and cold water pipes.

The two big tubs had fume hoods, tapering up into rounded brass flues, which fitted into a larger wall flue. The hoods now were up, lifted by sprocket wheels and chains. When there was any reason—any chemical like fuming nitric acid being used, for instance—the hoods could be lowered to fit snugly over the tubs, and thus conduct odors and poisonous gases out of the room's atmosphere.

Just what use this variety of apparatus could have in a studio-laboratory ordinarily devoted to architecture and optical physics, Masters failed to imagine. His training and imagination did not falter over one *other* possibility, however!

He could guess one possible use for slaking lime, nitric acid, and a fume-hooded vat... a shivery, significant thought in relation to Fernycroft, where men had taken to disappearing without trace....

For fifteen minutes then the detective paid close attention to the pair of tubs. At the end of that time he left the laboratory with the sack and carboy wrapped in a piece of newspaper. He gave the package to Captain Hainey, with a request to have it placed in the police safe.

"Something important, Jigger?" asked the officer, who seemed to have regained his temper partially. A number of early visits to the anisette bottle might have had something to do with his improved mental state; for certainly Leslie Blodgett had been going strong all morning thus far.

"Yes, this will be important evidence, I believe," Masters assured him gravely. "Just in case anything unexpected happens, remember I found them in Braithwaite's laboratory. And that they probably help explain the mysterious disappearance of Nathan Ertz!"

"Oh—my gosh, what *are* they?" Hainey's eyes grew round. He held the package with exaggerated care.

"I'd rather you didn't ask just now—or open the wrappings," said Jigger grimly. "I'll have something more to add

to them shortly, I'm afraid. I'm going to run over to Riverhead after a plumber!"

In the Studebaker, the errand took only a half hour. The
detective returned to the laboratory with the plumber, a
mustached man in overalls. The latter carried the usual kit
of tools, and also a number of cans with screw tops.

Fernycroft, being situated far from the town limits of
Riverhead and Greenport, of course had its own artesian
well. Water from this was pumped into tanks in two of
the towers, thence to be piped down by gravity to all the
faucets. The waste pipes led out to underground settling
tanks. The laboratory, being apart from the main building,
had its own small septic tank, little used.

Masters had the plumber detach the grease traps
from beneath the metal sinks, carefully scraping out the
encrusted accumulations found there. Then these traps
were replaced, and the two went out into the yard. There
the cover of the settling tank was removed, and the screw-
topped cans filled with a nauseous skimming of the liquid
found there.

This finished the job as far as the plumber was concerned.
Masters sent him out to the Studebaker with the slimy
samples, telling him to wait and get a lift back to his shop.

Masters himself went into the main part of Fernycroft,
and found Blodgett contemplating with vast satisfaction a
"secret cabinet" he had discovered in the downstairs hall. It
was a tall, slender panel which clicked open at the pressure
of a wall button. It was empty.

"Ha! Masters! Cast an eye over this!" bade the district
attorney, rubbing his hands with satisfaction. "The dimen-
sions are exactly—" he dropped his voice to a stage whis-

per—"exactly six feet by two feet by eighteen inches of depth! Doesn't that strike you as significant?"

"I'm sure of it!" agreed Masters solemnly. "Exactly the dimension of a coffin—or an umbrella cabinet, eh? But all nonsense aside, Blodgett, when is the inquest on Browne? And will you want me? I have a little work to do. It will take me back to my office for a day or so."

The district attorney glared at the thought of calling his secret cabinet a mere repository for umbrellas, but snapped out the information that the inquest would be held next morning at nine o'clock, and that the medical examiner certainly would insist upon Masters' presence.

The detective shrugged and turned to the door.

IN THE MOST prominent part of the Grand Central Palace in New York City, four porters emerged from behind a tarpaulin screen which had been raised to shield Braithwaite's work. Then came Vandervoort, and lastly the architect himself, mopping his forehead with a handkerchief and grinning a trifle shakily. The skyscraper model was safely in place!

A small crowd of spectators who were wandering around gazing at the other models that had already been entered, watched curiously as the porters, under Braithwaite's direction, removed the tarpaulin screen.

On a tall pedestal of black, all by itself, stood revealed the eight-foot show model, white and glittering!

Braithwaite raised one hand in signal. From two points high up in the exhibition room, spotlights sputtered and flared into white brilliance. Their beams converged upon the shining silver mirrors of the tower, emulating the sun which would shine upon the great building to be made on this plan. And the light was diffused so it did not dazzle the human eye, and reflected downward into the faces of the milling crowd below.

The drone of voices in that vast vault of a room ceased as if by magic, to be replaced by quick-drawn breaths long held. Those below stood almost still, and gazed upward at the skyscraper of the future....

AT THAT MOMENT, out in the laboratory of his combined residence and office, at Biskra Harbor, Jigger Masters drew out a broad slide from beneath his low-power microscope. On the glass lay a thin, wraithlike sliver, translucent as a codfish bone. The sliver was two-thirds of an inch in length.

"What would you say this thing was, Mitsui?" asked the detective, holding the slide up before the white-smocked Jap who was helping him, and lifting the sliver with slender forceps.

Mitsui gazed down impassively. "No can say," he admitted with a shake of his head. "Las' bit of lollypop, maybe?"

"Good imagination," approved Masters grimly. "But no, Mitsui. This happens to be human tissue—what's left of human bone after it has been acted upon by lime and acid. It's very nearly impossible to be sure, but I surmise two things. First, that this is the ghost of *the second bone of a man's little finger!* And second, that the little finger belonged to one of the two men who disappeared out there at Fernycroft!

"Grim humor, don't you think, to liquefy one of their victims and flush him down a drain, when they had a nice, shiny hearse so handy?"

13

THE CHEMICAL DEMON

THAT EVENING WHEN Marshall Vandervoort arrived at Biskra Harbor, he was pink-cheeked from the long ride out in his open car. "Whew! A ride in an open car in this weather is like holding your nose against an ice-berg, but it sure sets the old red blood pumping," he said, taking off his gloves. "Well, Chief, what is the news? It strikes me you must be pretty near the end of this string—though I, for one, can't see where we are, until we get hold of LeNarre, anyhow." He waited expectantly.

The detective nodded, leading the way back inside the two-story brick cottage which served as office and also as living quarters for himself and Mitsui. He went to the laboratory, with Vandervoort following. There he showed him the sliver of bone, and the other slight but unmistakable traces of acid-corroded and quicklime-eaten human tissue.

"These all came from the vat drains of Braithwaite's laboratory," he told him. "I'm sure you see the point."

"You mean it's—Ertz!" gasped Vandervoort. "My God, you don't mean that Braithwaite himself really did all these things? Killed his third secretary too, and washed him down the sink!"

"This case will be a good puzzle for you to figure out, Vandervoort," returned Masters with a dry smile. "You know everything now that I know. Beware of hasty conclusions, though. We are not yet at the end of the case. I must warn you, though, that I see a definite light now. We have much to do. I have been busy on the phone part of this afternoon, and have smoothed the way. But first, how about the skyscraper model?"

Vandervoort took out a cigarette and lighted it. "The model is up, and I'll say it looks like a crown jewel alongside them other entries, Chief!"

"That's excellent," returned Masters, nodding approvingly. "And, I guess that's about all we can do tonight. But tomorrow morning, first thing, I want you to scoot over to Montclair, New Jersey. That's the home town of Louis LeNarre, the missing secretary of Isaac Abeles, I've found out."

"But the powder plant people said they had been phoning everywhere, and—"

"I know," rejoined Masters with a slight frown. "He probably isn't anywhere. This is a bad winter for private secretaries. But I phoned around and found out that his family used to live in Montclair. More than likely the town photographers have a picture of him. Or else some girl he used to trot around with… anyway, I *must* have a picture of him, and just as soon as possible! If you don't succeed in Montclair, you'll have to dash up to Amherst, where he went to college. Maybe there will be a picture in a year book, or a frat group. Montclair sounds like a better bet to me, though. Let me hear from you just the instant you have that picture. And above all, when you *do* get it, don't make any public comments on what it may cause you to think!"

From Vandervoort's expression it was evident that his
brain was racing, yet vastly puzzled. "I'm going to think this
out!" he asserted, with a jutting of the chin. "But I must be
pretty dumb, because I can't figure out—"

Crash! Thump!

Something heavy struck the lower pane of glass in one
of the six windows of the long, narrow laboratory. With a
tinkle the glass shattered, and a rattling roar announced the
shade running up on its roller. At the same instant something heavy was hurled in through the aperture, striking
the cork carpet of the floor and sliding. The three men,
in the split-second following the crash, jerked about and
stared.

In the window appeared for a brief fraction of time, the
spectacled, contorted face of *Nathan Ertz!*

QUICK AS HE could jam one hand into his jacket pocket,
and yank forth his automatic, Masters fired. Then he leaped
toward the window, peered out, and fired again.

"Damn! Missed..." he grated, then swung about, the
smoking pistol in his hand. "Keep away from that!" he
yelled. Vandervoort was bending toward the object which
had come through the window. "It's a bomb! *Run!*"

Had that innocent-appearing brown leather Boston
bag contained a bomb of any ordinary explosive variety,
all three men must have suffered. But it did not go off in
the manner of dynamite or black powder. Instead, after the
one faint, muffled *plop* which had been almost drowned
out by the sound made by its impact on the floor, the bag
remained quiescent. It rapidly puffed out, ballooning
until all the creases in the leather sides were distended
and smooth.

Then—*zzzzzzz!*

From a dozen cracks or other apertures at once, a cloud of grayish vapor shot forth into the laboratory!

Vandervoort, stopped in the act of reaching for it, leaped backward with a yell, just managing to evade a jet of the gas. He, Mitsui, and Masters darted to the other windows, threw the sashes high, then ran for the door. When this was thrown open it created an outward draft. They could stay there and watch the curious thing that happened.

The leather bag melted, disintegrated before their eyes! Fuming, rolling vapor then obscured the place where it had been. The vapor was wafted toward the windows, but it was being generated far too fast to be content with that. It filled the room. Masters at last was compelled to close the door, and lead his companions away. His face was stern, frowning.

"I don't know just what that is, but stay away from it!" he bade curtly. "Doesn't look like hydrocyanic, arsine, phosgene, or any of the other war gases. Besides, it ate right through leather so fast… H'mmm! Say, Vandervoort, take this gun. Go outside, but not too near those windows. Watch for *fire!* I don't think our Mr. Ertz is still in the neighborhood. But if you see him again, *now or ever,* shoot on sight!"

The eager assistant no more had reached the patch of frozen lawn outside, than a yell burst from his lips.

"Fire! It's afire, Jigger!" He looked, mystified and appalled at the murky tongues of flame which came rushing out of the windows of the laboratory.

Inside, Masters coolly called the Biskra Harbor Fire Department, asking for the chemical wagon. "A foamite spray will do the most good," he advised, and hung up. Three seconds later came the mournful bellow of the fire siren.

Since the walls of the laboratory were fireproofed, the conflagration did not amount to much as a spectacle. When the fire chief rushed up in his little red car with gong clanging, Masters advised him instantly that poison gas was involved. Therefore the foamite line was manned by men in masks, and the smothering chemical played through a window.

In one minute after that the fire was out, though no one ventured inside until next morning. In a room upstairs, Masters explained to Vandervoort hurriedly.

"It was fluorine, or rather, hydrofluoric acid—what scientists call 'the chemical fury.' It is by far the most terrible gas known to man, almost as swift to act, if inhaled, as hydrocyanic acid. Otherwise, though, it makes prussic acid seem as harmless by comparison as a bottle of milk.

"One drop on the bare skin is enough to insure a man's death in fiendish agony! The poison goes all through the system, open sores come and spread. But why enlarge on that? We were all lucky to get out of reach of the fumes."

"How did Ertz work it?" demanded Vandervoort. "That *was Ertz*—I'd know him anywhere! But he just didn't bring it loose in that Boston bag, of course?"

"Naturally not. Of course we can never guess, from what remains, just how it was done. The details of it, I mean. But hydrofluoric has to be made right where it is used, because there is nothing on God's green earth that will hold it for long. Glass is eaten through as swiftly as that leather bag you saw. Gold, even paraffin bottles, the same. A platinum flask, costing several thousand dollars, would hold it for a little while—but would be totally changed into platinum fluoride in a few hours. Destroyed, in other words. No, men have yet to learn how to handle that chemical demon!

"But they do know how to make it, easily enough. Cryolite combined with sulphuric acid will do it. I think our dear friend Ertz simply put several pounds of the mineral cryolite into his Boston bag, along with a fragile flask of strong sulphuric acid.

"Throwing the bag to the floor, broke the flask. The acid flooded over the cryolite, instantly making hydrofluoric acid gas. This expanded hugely, of course, ate through the leather, and flooded the laboratory."

"But what started the fire, Chief? You seemed to know beforehand that it was coming."

"Fluorine pure or in this acid form has the property of setting any number of ordinary chemicals ablaze," said Masters. "I had a lot of different chemicals on the shelves— some unstoppered." The detective frowned, seemed to be thinking. "Oh, by the way, before you go, Vandervoort, put in a call for Braithwaite, out at Ferny croft."

Vandervoort nodded, and went out to the extension phone in the hall. A few minutes later he returned, shaking his head.

"I got Martha Karnett, Chief," he reported. "She said Braithwaite hasn't got back from New York yet. Any message to leave?"

"No, none," said Jigger Masters grimly. "I hope, though, that he *does* get back! There have been just about enough people die or disappear from that infernal House of the Damned!"

14

WITCH FIRES BURNING

CHESTER ALWYN BRAITHWAITE did not return to Fernycroft that night, but no one had cause to worry. A few minutes before ten o'clock the phone rang at Fernycroft. Martin King, the butler, answered and heard the voice of his master on long distance.

"I can't get back tonight, Martin," said the architect grumpily. "Missed the 9:29, and that's the last Greenport train. Pack me a change of clothes, and bring it in on the early morning train. I'm staying tonight at the Carrington. Yes, yes, the gray tweeds will be all right…"

So the butler, with no more than a momentary grimace of regret for the change in the easy-going employer who had once called him familiarly "Rex" and treated him more nearly as a human being, went back and reassured the Karnetts.

Pierre, the cook, was becoming more and more grumpy. Nobody in this house of tragedy had time any longer to appreciate a well-cooked dinner. *Nom d'un chien,* no!

Lucy Borden had quit. Too many things had happened recently to get on her nerves.

Martha Karnett continued to knit placidly. She was a little quieter, perhaps. Joe Karnett, her husband, slouched

around his daily chores with the electric light plant, the
cars, the vacuum cleaner. He too had grown even surlier,
if possible.

And the Dark Shade of Death that hovered over Fernycroft Mansion prepared for yet another visit to a member
of its household.

THE COUNTRY COURTHOUSE-JAIL at Riverhead was all
in darkness, save for one ceiling light in the upstairs office.
There Sergeant Finn dozed peacefully, his number thirteen
brogans cocked up on a corner of the ancient roll-top desk.

In the basement cell tier, one prisoner slept. The next
morning he was due to appear at the inquest on the body
of his erstwhile companion at Fernycroft, Stonewall J.
Browne; but it did not bother his conscience. There were
no other prisoners in the jail this night.

The iron-barred windows of the cells rose three feet
above the ground level, a semi-circular well in front of each
window admitting a trifle more light than that which came
in directly. In the cell where Dr. Spinelli lay face down
upon his cot, the window was open a foot at the top for
ventilation. The scientist always granted himself plenty of
fresh air, even in winter.

A solitary man walked swiftly and without noise
through the streets of the sleeping village. He came to the
courthouse yard, and here took to the grass; As he came
opposite the row of cell windows he stopped, back against
the bole of a tree. He pulled down the military collar of his
greatcoat a little, so he could hear more plainly.

Only one sound broke the stillness of the chilly night.
In the end cell, the one with the window open, a prisoner

snored nasally, uneasily. He made a blubbery sound with his lips as he exhaled.

After ten minutes of vigil, the man in the greatcoat tip-toed forward. He leaned forward over the iron rail which guarded the window wells to prevent children or animals from falling down them.

As the visitor's eyes accustomed themselves to the darkness inside the cell beyond the bars, he saw a vague shape lying there, shrouded in blankets. On a pillow on the farthest end of the bed, was the darker splotch of a human head.

Reaching under his greatcoat, the newcomer brought out a pistol with a long silencer attached. It was one of those automatics of foreign make with square stock and long, slender barrel. Leveling this, resting it upon the iron rail for greater accuracy, the stranger leaned down, squinted, squeezed the trigger once... twice...

The only sound was a *chuff*... *chuff*... two smothered sneezes.

Inside the cell Dr. Spinelli twitched violently once. An arm raised, then fell limply down beside the cot. Then the snores ceased. All was quiet.

The man in the greatcoat tiptoed away, vanishing in the direction he had come. Upstairs in the police station, Sergeant Finn dozed on undisturbed...

DR. SPINELLI WAS stiff, his cot soaked with blood, when they found him at breakfast time next morning. One bullet from a .38 had notched his skull above his right ear; but it had been the second slug of lead, the one that had crashed through his back and lodged against his ribs near his heart, which caused death.

The manner of shooting through the open window was plain enough. Only there was no trace at all of the killer. He had left no footprints in the grass or gravel, no fingerprints upon the iron rail. There had been no train leaving Riverhead until the 5:21 A.M. Because of the winter season, there had not been a single male passenger on this, the only rider of either sex being one colored woman who was quitting her job and going back to Brooklyn.

The tragic news reached Masters at Biskra Harbor just as he was about to set forth in the car with Mitsui, for the inquest. Braithwaite was reached by phone at the Hotel Carrington. He said he expected Martin King with his clothes almost any minute, and would take the first train back to Riverhead after the butler arrived.

Out at the county seat confusion reigned. The plans of District Attorney Blodgett, abetted by Captain Hainey and the youthful, rural deputy sheriff, Conkling, were rendered absurd. The prime suspect, the man against whom all of the murders save that of Peter Unger would have been charged, lay dead in his cell. The murderer had been too contemptuous of the authorities even to give them a way to save face. He might have done that readily enough, by tossing the gun in through the window. Even with an entire absence of fingermarks, and with no explanation of how a .38 revolver had been overlooked when Dr. Spinelli was searched by the county police, District Attorney Blodgett would have seized eagerly enough upon the explanation of remorse and suicide. It would have simplified matters so tremendously!

With no trace of a gun in the cell, however, the ugly fact of another murder had to be faced.

Masters, pale and grim, had little to say. He did not

reproach anyone, despite the fact that he had foreseen just this tragic possibility, and had so warned Hainey. The whole case, in a way, was a reproach to himself. Should he not have contrived some means of guarding these people?

The inquest was not held until two o'clock in the afternoon, and then it was a dismal farce. Instead of the definite arraignment of Dr. Leo Spinelli as a suspect to be put on trial for his life, the evidence was limited to the definite facts of murder. The whole proceedings in the inquest over Static Browne took only three-quarters of an hour, and the jury did not leave their seats. They whispered together a moment, and then returned the rubber-stamp verdict that Stonewall J. (Static) Browne had been murdered by a person or persons unknown.

Masters left Riverhead shortly after that, stopping only for one savage bit of advice to Hainey.

"If you don't want more of the same to happen, Captain," Jigger said in a low, tense voice, "keep some of your men on guard at Fernycroft! The servants and Braithwaite himself are the people you want to watch. My assistant and I are on the spot next, I think. But there seems no logical reason why the murderer should not start on the few people left alive in that Damned House!"

"Damned is right!" admitted Hainey shakily. "All right, Jigger. I'll go myself, and take a squad of men—though this has gone so far I don't see how just guarding anybody is going to help. Hell, they kill 'em off even when they're in jail cells!"

But Masters had turned on his heel, and was striding out to his waiting car.

"New York *Register* Building—42nd Street!" he directed

Mitsui. The Jap nodded imperturbably. A second after the door closed, the Studebaker was on its hundred-mile way westward. In ten minutes it was on the main highway, droning along at a comfortable sixty-five miles per hour. Stretching his long legs forward, Masters closed his eyes and relaxed. He even slept a little, until the car reached the traffic lights of Greater New York.

Before reaching the old newspaper building, Masters dismissed the car, telling Mitsui to garage the car at their usual place on 41st Street, and walked into the Grand Central Palace. Here he entered the main exhibition room, and stood for two minutes looking at the model of Braithwaite's skyscraper, there in the front rank of the contest exhibit.

The spotlights on the mirrors were marvellously effective.

"There just isn't any other entry!" reflected Masters. "Compared to this, the others don't even exist."

He watched the spectators who entered the big building. Without exception people stopped at first sight, and gazed. Some made audible comment, wondering and appreciative. Some few were scornful, but most looked upon the model and the project it represented as something startling and yet undeniably beautiful.

AT THE DILAPIDATED old fire-trap which still housed the New York *Register,* Masters identified himself to an assistant city editor—a hardboiled man who became almost obsequious on learning that this was the Jigger Masters who was handling the Fernycroft investigations.

But Masters would state his business to only one man.

"I have to talk to Spencer Dean," he told the eye-shaded

assistant editor. "You can tell him I have the greatest crime story in all your newspaper's history—perhaps!"

McNamara whistled. "Exclusive too, eh?" he mocked.

"It ought to be," returned Masters grimly. "I think it concerns the whole future of this paper!"

The tall, gaunt, white-haired Spencer Dean received Jigger Masters with quiet, old-fashioned courtesy. Somehow this veteran publisher kept a calm heart and mind even in the midst of the high-keyed tumult of a metropolitan daily newspaper office.

"Have a chair and help yourself to cigars," invited Dean, when a brief handclasp was finished. He placed a box at Jigger's elbow, but the latter shook his head, and lighted a cigarette. "I have had the pleasure of following two of your cases—and thorough jobs they were," continued Dean, leaning back in his swivel chair and lighting a Panatella. "Is this affair out at Fernycroft coming to a head? I know that you lately have been handling it out there."

"Handling it is scarcely the correct phrase," explained Masters quietly. "I have merely been retained as a private investigator, but the police have been very generous with their assistance. But the reason I came to see you, Mr. Dean, is that the affair seems to have become linked up with the *Register!* At least, I suspect that very strongly."

"What? The *Register!* You mean—through the model Braithwaite submitted to our contest? I—you are aware, of course, that the contest has not officially closed? I cannot discuss anything—"

Masters quickly disposed of any suspicion of his own motives. "What merit or lack of merit there may be in Mr. Braithwaite's plan and model, is completely beside the question," he said. "At least for the present, it is—and we're dealing with an emergency. Multiple murder! And my sole object in coming to you here, is to ask your cooperation in stopping the red-handed devil who is committing it!"

"Good. Any decent citizen would grant such a request, of course. Now tell me, how can I—and the New York *Register*—do more than has been done? I suppose you know we sent our three best crime reporters out there this morning?"

"Two of them, plus your own cooperation in silence until I am ready to prove the case, will do the trick—if I am right, of course," said Masters quietly. "Here is the position—"

Briefly and rapidly he sketched happenings thus far in the Fernycroft enigma, giving each of the incidents an interpretation suited to the theory which now drove him relentlessly toward the end.

"I can prove myself right or wrong, but in order to do so, I shall have to take that show model of Braithwaite's out of its place at Grand Central. Yes, yes, just a moment!" he added, when unmistakable signs of negation began to show on Spencer Dean's countenance. "Since the contest closes at midnight, Monday, couldn't the committee in charge of the grand prize award decide to remove five or six of the showier models, to your display advertising window down-stairs? And then bring Braithwaite's up here?"

"H'm-mm—it might be done," agreed-the newspaper publisher hesitatingly. "But go on. Tell me just what you propose."

Masters nodded, tamping out his cigarette. For fifteen minutes then he talked earnestly. At the end of that time he had the satisfaction of hearing Spencer Dean give orders for two of his reporters to come back from Riverhead and Fernycroft. He himself would instruct them in the duties respecting a "drive-it-yourself" automobile which Masters believed must have been used, and then regarding the other architects who had been at the Grand Central with their respective models.

With these two branches of investigation adequately covered by men whose bread and butter depended upon their discreet silence, Masters believed that he, with Marshall Vandervoort, could handle all the rest.

On leaving the serious-faced newspaper publisher, Masters hurried over to a theatrical costumer's on 44th Street. There he made one purchase of a pair of shell-rimmed spectacles, lensed with plain glass. He also looked over racks which held several hundred wigs of different shapes and colors.

None of these exactly suited, though one brownish affair with a back-center part after the Continental style, was reasonably close to requirements. Masters selected and paid for this, but then left it with the costumer, asking that two small changes be made in the wig. Vandervoort would call for it the next evening, Saturday.

That night, back in Biskra Harbor, Masters told Vandervoort about the arrangements he had made, though without explaining the full reasons. Perhaps all this appalling surmise, this structure of theory, would fall flat as unleavened bread. In which case Jigger Masters preferred to have only the blame of his own conscience.

Vandervoort had one bit of news. Isaac Abeles, president of the Upton Flat Powder Company, had reached town.

Worried about his secretary, Louis LeNarre, he had flown up from Miami. He now was at Madison, Connecticut, and would like to have Mr. Masters communicate with him.

"I suppose he wants you to start a hunt for LeNarre," suggested Vandervoort.

"Perhaps," said Masters thoughtfully. "By the way, did you get hold of that photograph of LeNarre I asked you to try to get in Montclair?"

Vandervoort shook his head. "Not yet. But I've got one coming. I found a photographer who used to make pictures for the LeNarre family. He didn't have any prints, but's got an original negative of LeNarre—you know most photographers save their plates in case a customer ever wants any extra prints made. He is making a new print for us and will send it right along the minute it is finished."

At that moment the doorbell rang. Vandervoort answered it. "Hello—here it is now, I guess," he said, as he signed for a special delivery parcel.

A moment later he and Masters were bending over, cutting the cord and unwrapping the stout paper that protected the picture.

As the face in the picture came to the light, Vandervoort gave a startled exclamation. "My God—!"

Masters merely nodded his head, staring away into the distance. His face was grim, deathly so. "I thought so. Just a little thing, a photograph. But it can send a man as quick to his death as that gallon of nitroglycerine sent poor Barnes."

FROM THE MOMENT the photograph came until the following Tuesday, when Masters had made plans with Spencer Dean for the final evidence, the days of both Masters and Vandervoort were crowded with action.

Masters had to see both Isaac Abeles and Spencer Dean. He had to tell them both some of the latest things he had discovered.

Abeles, in particular, received the news with a shock. LeNarre was a relative by marriage, and one of the most brilliant minds the old powder manufacturer had ever met. "I don't believe it—I can't!" he cried dazedly. But he agreed to be present, with Dean and the others, at the *Register* office on Monday and Tuesday as Masters requested.

Meantime, on Sunday and Monday, the two *Register* reporters assigned to run down the drive-it-yourself car had come in with their report, and also with such information as they had been able to gather from other exhibitors in Grand Central Palace.

Spencer Dean had meanwhile had four or five of the showier prize models moved from Grand Central Palace to the *Register* building on Monday. It was still short of midnight on Monday when Dean, Masters, Abeles, Vandervoort, and two reporters uncrated the gleaming model of Braithwaite's skyscraper and turned it gently on its side.

Masters immediately set to Work with a thin, broad-bladed chisel. He followed the line of jointure between the two halves. And with smaller difficulty than expected, he succeeded in effecting a clean cleavage.

Both halves were laid on their backs then, in the identical position they had been while still in the molds in the Fernycroft studio-laboratory, drying out.

All the men crowded around, studying closely the surfaces revealed. Then Abeles straightened with a snort.

"You see!" he scoffed. "Dere is no sign at all!"

"I'm sorry to say you're wrong!" retorted the detective. "Look at this!" With one finger he indicated a faint line which appeared on one half of the plaster model. This line was very noticeable down in the wider part which represented the lower portion of the skyscraper, but also continued upward well into the bottom of the mirrored tower.

"Now watch!"

With the chisel he gently chipped along the faint line for a distance of two feet. Then, raising the heel of his right hand, he struck a sudden downward blow.

Up came a long flake of plaster, raised by the chisel edge!

A gasp came from all their throats. Even the hard-boiled Vandervoort paled from his usual ruddy complexion at the terrible thing revealed. "Good Lord of Love!" he said.

"You see," said Masters with grim quietness, "Braithwaite explained one time that Nathan Ertz *could not* have gone away voluntarily! He was to have shared in the reward—the prize—*if* it was won by this model! *He had a strong proprietary interest* in *the model!*"

15

BEHIND THE MASK

CHESTER ALWYN BRAITHWAITE decided that his nerve could stand no more.

"I'm sorry, Martin," he told the butler, when he arrived home after the trip to Riverhead and a long talk with the police about the latest tragedy, "but I can't let these things go on any longer. Just as soon as I can do so, after the inquest on poor Doctor Spinelli, I'm going to close up Fernycroft. I'll probably sell it, if I ever get a chance—though who would want to come out and live here, I can't imagine."

"Then you mean you won't have any more use for me—for us? The Karnetts, Pierre, and myself?"

"I'm afraid not. I'll pay you each six months' salary, of course. But I intend to live quietly in a New York hotel, until after the *Register* contest is decided. Then probably I'll travel in Italy and France. I may get a valet and chauffeur over there, but I won't try to keep house anywhere."

THROUGH THE HOURS of investigation, and then the new inquest on the body of Dr. Spinelli on Saturday, Braithwaite was courteous as always toward the police, troopers and others. Yet a frown showed often on his forehead. It was plain, too, that being guarded by Hainey and several of his men was not pleasant. Being under actual arrest and detention had not saved Browne and Spinelli from disagreeable ends. What did Hainey think he could do for Braithwaite?

Sunday evening he got in touch with Masters by phone, exhibiting petulance. What had the detective to report? Had anything at all been accomplished? Braithwaite said that he wanted to get away from Fernycroft now, and was willing to pay any reasonable bill of the detective agency. As far as he, Chester Braithwaite, could see, however, nothing at all had been accomplished. He was just as far as ever from exoneration in the eyes of Miss Sylvia Reese and her father; and there was no telling what the public at large thought of him.

"I tell you, Mr. Masters, I have been calm enough thus far; but I'm beginning to get the jitters now, myself." He told of his intention of closing up Fernycroft at the end of the following week. "And meanwhile," he asked in conclusion, "can't I be rid of these police that are quartered out here? They make me more uneasy, rather than more reassured."

Masters' tone sounded grave, even hopeless over the wire. "I feel too badly about all this, Mr. Braithwaite, to bill you for my own services," he said. "The work of my subordinates, of course, is a different matter. I shall make it a point to see you sometime this week. And I can only reiterate my regrets that this case has turned out as it has. The police will probably not stay forever at Fernycroft, but I think you will have to put up with them a little while longer."

Braithwaite seemed about to say something more, but

evidently changed his mind. As he replaced the receiver, a look of scorn twisted his face. So this was the great Jigger Masters! Perhaps an able enough fellow, when pitted against small-time criminals, nitwits. Helpless, though, when a real artist in plotting led him about by the nose....

He could not see along the miles of telephone wire to Biskra Harbor where the despised detective stood quite a full minute after the end of the call. The face of Masters was craggy and harsh. His narrowed eyes burned with a light which was like the deadly sparkle from a razor-sharp blade or the cold, green glint from an iceberg's depths.

EARLY TUESDAY MORNING Captain Hainey and his men departed, saying nothing. Braithwaite drew a long breath of relief. With the help of Martin King he set about the job of packing up. He would stay no longer in Fernycroft.

There came a pleasant interruption. Spencer Dean, editor and publisher of the New York *Register,* phoned at a quarter of eleven. Braithwaite stiffened and drew a long breath, while he listened. A slow smile started on his countenance. Spencer Dean was speaking for the judges. Though the contest had not been definitely decided it was obvious to everyone that Mr. Braithwaite's magnificent skyscraper design would have to be among those finally considered.

"The point is this," said Dean. "I am betraying no confidences in saying that the judges will have to put some questions to you, especially in regard to the mirror arrangement, before they feel they can evaluate your ideas correctly. Would you find it convenient to drop down to my office this afternoon, say at three o'clock or three-thirty?"

Braithwaite chuckled. "I'll try my best," he promised,

"though this is pretty short notice. I'll probably have to drive in. So if I'm a little late, don't despair."

He turned away from the phone, whistling cheerfully. This was a faster bit of action than he had even dared to hope for. But it was evident that no more than one good look had been necessary for the judges to realize the merit of his entry.

Despite the speed of the big Lancia, there was nothing to do but take it slowly when they came to the narrow bottleneck for traffic on the western end of Long Island. But Braithwaite was still jaunty when he gave his card to a cynical youth at the information desk, and asked to see Spencer Dean. While he waited, Braithwaite glanced about disparagingly at the walls of the battered, out-of-date building which had housed the *Register* for two generations. If they waited much longer before they erected their new building, the old one would probably crumble to bits beneath them.

The hands of Braithwaite's wrist-watch showed exactly four o'clock, as the office boy returned to guide him to Spencer Dean's twelfth-floor office. The youth stole scared, sidewise glances at the caller, but Braithwaite just then was too jubilant to notice. Everything was coming his way. It was a just reward, too. He deserved everything!

A series of shocks awaited him in Dean's office. The first one halted him just inside the doorway. Dean himself, grave of face, arose to welcome the visitor. With him, surprisingly enough, was Jigger Masters! But this was not the great shock which stiffened Braithwaite, caused him to go pale and search his brain swiftly, fiercely for a possible explanation.

Up here in Spencer Dean's office stood his model skyscraper! Shiny and immaculate, it stood alone at one side of the long desk behind which Dean and Masters had been seated!

"Why—you've got it here!" breathed Braithwaite. "Why?"

"Oh, the model," nodded Dean negligently. "Yes, we thought it advisable to have it for this conference. It has—"

He was interrupted. The door opened, and a crowd of people entered, some of the men carrying office chairs, which they set down in rows, facing the white model. Braithwaite, Dean and Masters had to retreat toward the long desk, where the newspaper publisher indicated a leather-upholstered chair for the architect.

"There will be quite a crowd here," he said off-handedly. "If you'd just sit here... He turned the chair sidewise, so it also faced the tower of mirrors.

The millionaire architect, however, made no move to accept. He stood straight and pale, staring in a kind of petrified horror at the people who came in. These were not judges—of the contest, at least!

First came three men, each with four wooden chairs. Trooper Carey, Vandervoort, and Captain Hainey! Then three more State troopers in uniform; men who looked sternly out of level eyes at Braithwaite, and whose glances he found it suddenly difficult to meet!

Chairs, more chairs! All arranged in rows, like seats in a classroom—or a court!

The architect's brain was reeling. Instead of coming down to talk pleasantly, half-patronizingly to a group of earnest boobs who would treat him in turn with the profound respect due a genius, Braithwaite saw that for him there was something decidedly different on the program. Why, this was a trap! He started toward the door, but stopped after one pace. The two troopers waiting there had quietly stepped into the doorway as if forming a barrier to all egress!

It *was* a trap! What on earth did they know?

Into the room still streamed people. Each one, practically, sent a new wave of gooseflesh across the architect's forearms. Dr. Elbert Reese with Sylvia on his arm—and both trying not to look in his direction! Martin King and all the Karnetts! Why, they must have commandeered one of the other cars, and driven like mad, in order to get here so soon after Braithwaite's Lancia! Only Pierre, the cook, was missing out of the ordinary household at Fernycroft... and it was easy to guess that the French chef had not been brought, because of his somewhat limited knowledge of English.

A group of five people from Montclair, New Jersey, among them a commercial photographer....

Lastly came a chunky, slightly pompous, gray-haired man in the company of a lean, grim-faced fellow six feet three or more in height. With an inner gasp, Chester Braithwaite gave up hope. These two last comers were Isaac Abeles and Pickell, his superintendent of the Lipton Flat Powder Company!

As these people settled themselves in the waiting chairs, Braithwaite also seated himself. He was pale, but calm now. His eyes strayed to the windows at his right. One of these stood open about a foot. Below there was the hum of 42nd Street.

"A strange group of contest judges!" said Braithwaite dryly to Masters, who sat between him and Spencer Dean.

"Oh, didn't Dean tell you?" asked the detective with a lift of the dark eyebrows. "There seems to be a certain misunderstanding in respect to this model—as to just who actually *is* submitting it! A sort of accusation of copying or stolen ideas. But now I see we can come to order—"

"I won't stay to listen to any such nonsense!" snapped Braithwaite. He started to rise and go out, but again the pair of troopers at the door met his eyes with unwavering determination, and he shrugged. No one had bothered to answer him. Well, he would stay, after all—for a while, anyhow. Perhaps it might not be as bad as he feared.

It was to be far worse.

THERE WAS NO preparatory word of any sort. Spencer Dean held up one hand. A hush fell upon the assemblage. And Sylvia Reese stood up. Her face was white, but her lips were tight and determined. She was looking straight at the architect now.

"To the best of my knowledge, *this man* looks almost like—like Chester Braithwaite," she said in a low, broken voice. "But— *But he is not the real Chester Braithwaite!*"

"What—!" cried one of the reporters amazedly. "Not the *real* Chester Braithwaite—?" But Spencer Dean silenced him with a glare, and turned back to the girl grimly. "Would you mind telling us all how you know this, Miss Reese?"

"I know it for several reasons; knew it the moment I saw and heard this—this imposter! Certain vague mannerisms—little tones of the voice. But I can prove it in one moment, sir, if this person will answer one question." She suddenly turned the full gaze of her eyes upon the man in the leather chair. "Tell me, sir, how you met me first—*if you ever met me!*"

Braithwaite was white-faced. But still Masters had to admire his grip on his nerves, his supreme control. "I do not quite see the object of this assemblage," he announced, his lips curling contemptuously. "If there is any irregularity in respect to my model skyscraper, I am willing to discuss that. But as to the preposterous imputation of this woman—" He shrugged his shoulders. "I have no intention of discussing my relations with women, in public."

"You beast!" cried the girl. "I never met the real Chester Braithwaite in my life under conditions I would be ashamed to reveal in public! Where I met him first was on a diving raft at Lake Onago, and your insinuations—"

But the grim-faced publisher had nodded to her father, and the minister reached over and drew his daughter back to her seat.

It was the butler, Martin King, who now stood up.

"Mr. Dean," he said respectfully, "ever since I have been back from my vacation in Canada, I have noticed queer changes in my master. He looks a little different, acts a little different—and he does not even call me by the same name he used to use." He swung suddenly upon the white-faced architect. "Mr. Braithwaite, what was your usual name for me?"

Braithwaite sat there silent, lips compressed. His gray eyes did not flinch before the accusing stares of the people who waited to hear his voice, however.

"I'll tell you what it was!" Martin King's words were crisp, clear. "You always called me 'Rex!' You said it meant 'King' in Latin!"

With that simple but dramatic pronouncement the butler sat down.

At that moment the outside door of the office opened, admitting two late arrivals. These were Leslie Blodgett, the district attorney of Suffolk, and the deputy sheriff, Conkling. Blodgett had grumbled savagely at having to waste time coming clear into New York; but now, giving one sniff at the air and one look at the people assembled, he evidently sensed the reality of the proceedings. He slumped down in a chair and fingered his felt hat nervously.

Masters spoke now, lifting up a cabinet photograph so that all might see.

"You will probably agree that this is a good likeness of the man who now calls himself Mr. Chester Braithwaite?" queried the detective.

A chorus of assent answered. Over this came the strident comment of the photographer brought from Montclair. "It sure ought to be! I took it! Only, his name wasn't Braithwaite then…."

The gray-haired, slightly pompous man arose then. "My name is Isaac Abeles," he said. "I am the president of the Upton Flat Powder Company. My superintendent is with me." He touched the shoulder of the tall, grim-faced fellow who had entered with him. For a second he hesitated, and then his voice continued, hoarse, anguished. "I would not believe it until I see it. But now I see it—and I got to believe! This man here is not got a right to the name Braithwaite at all! He is my cousin by marriage, and he is my own secretary. His name, it is Louis LeNarre! Should I know—ah-h-hh!"

He sat down, breathing heavily, his face wearing the

stricken look of the proud Jew whose kin has disgraced his race.

In the dead silence that followed, Masters reached out, opened a drawer in the desk, and brought out two articles which he placed casually on the desk in front of him. These were a pair of shellrimmed spectacles similar to those worn once by Nathan Ertz, and a brown wig a little gray at the temples. The wig showed a back-center part, after the Continental fashion.

For the first time fright flashed unmistakably into the countenance of Braithwaite. His gray eyes seemed to bulge as he stared down at the silently accusing bits of evidence.

But Masters did not speak of them just now. Instead, he leaned over and touched the architect on one arm.

"Tell us—" he said slowly and distinctly—"tell us, Mr. Louis LeNarre, alias Nathan Ertz, alias Chester Alwyn Braithwaite, just *what it was you concealed in the center of your model skyscraper?*"

"Eh? Eh? I don't—" gasped the harried man, half rising, then sinking part way back to sit rigidly upon the edge of his chair.

Masters gestured with one hand at the glittering skyscraper model. All eyes turned in that direction.

"The *real* Chester Braithwaite built this model," said Masters in a solemn voice. "His murderer was merciless— in all but one thing. *He let Mr. Braithwaite sign his work!*"

One of Masters' hands tugged at a cord beneath the desk. No one saw. What they did see, however—

The tower of mirrors was falling forward to the floor! *Crash!*

Half of the tower, and the model of the setback building below it, had split at the exact place Jigger Masters earlier had separated the parts. The front half fell with a brittle roar of breaking glass and plaster. But the rear half, the part Masters had so carefully explored with the chisel, still stood on its pedestal.

And there before the horrified eyes of the spectators, embedded in the white plaster like some prehistoric fossil in enshrouding rock, were the wraithlike, ghostly bones of a man!

Not a complete skeleton. Not even any single bone was complete. Yet ribs, spine, papery skull, thigh bones: they were all there, approximately in place though disarticulated. The acid and lime used by the murderer had eaten away much of their substance; yet enough remained so that every one of the people in that room knew that he or she looked upon what once had been a man!

A SUDDEN SHRIEK broke from the man who had called himself Braithwaite. Eyes wide, staring, he suddenly dove forward, grabbed up the spectacles and wig, and then ran to the partly open window at his right. He threw high the sash—scrambled up—

Then Masters' long arms reached him, fastening about his waist as he struggled and fought to throw himself from the height. Merciless hands hauled him back inside.

The man did not cease screaming now. Clawing, biting, rolling over, he fought insensately against the remorseless grip of strong arms.

The troopers had closed in now, stern, efficient, implacable men. There was the flash of metal. And with the click of the handcuffs about his wrists there seemed to come to the struggling man a realization that hope had fled. He ceased fighting, broke into hysterical tears.

"All right. You've got me—damn you!" he quavered.

"And so," said Masters, backing away and dabbing with a handkerchief at a bleeding cheek, "we come to the end of the terror at Fernycroft. Just to convince everyone of this man's impersonations, his criminal genius—"

He bent, picked up wig and spectacles from the floor where they had dropped, and then fitted them in place on the captive. The latter ducked, tried to squirm away, but Masters was remorseless.

"There!" said the detective with satisfaction. "Behold Mr. Louis LeNarre, who became Mr. Nathan Ertz, the secretary—for the purpose of murdering a millionaire, Chester Braithwaite, and taking his place! Do you wish to make a statement to that effect, Mr. LeNarre?"

"I—I want to speak to you, Masters—alone," gasped the prisoner, his whole body quivering, the perspiration standing out on his forehead in drops.

Masters gave the troopers a significant look. They fell back. Masters bent down over the manacled man.

"You— You've got me!" panted the prisoner. "I'll make a bargain with you—"

"A bargain? What sort of bargain?" returned Masters sharply. "A confession?"

"Yes."

"And what do you want me to do?"

"Nothing much. Only a—a little advertisement. In the newspapers."

"An advertisement, in the newspapers!" Masters could not repress an exclamation.

"Yes. Just in the 'personal' column. Will you?"

Masters was thoughtful for a moment, his keen eyes narrowed. Suddenly he nodded his head. "It's a bargain. Here—you can write it in my notebook right now." There was a moment's scribbling, impeded by the awkward handcuffs. Then Masters took a quick glance at what had been written, and put the notebook back in his pocket. "And now the confession?"

"You'll get it—when I read that notice in the *Register*, tomorrow!"

16

THE RED COLLECTORS

IN THE "AGONY" column of the New York *Register* next morning appeared a terse item, overlooked by most readers who had eyes only for the scarehead solutions of the Fernycroft enigma handed them in print and pictures on the first three pages.

Not even the *Register* connected the obscure, personal item, which Masters had sent in as soon as Captain Hainey and the troopers had whisked the prisoner away to Riverhead jail, with the front page story.

The personal item read:

R-C—Send capsule or will spill everything.

L.

Masters himself brought the morning paper to LeNarre in his cell. Yet even when he read the item, nodding his grim satisfaction, the prisoner was not quite ready to keep his end of the bargain.

"Not just yet, damn you," he snarled. "Oh yes, open that window before you go, will you? Maybe tonight I'll have ready the thing you want... if you'll leave pen and paper."

Masters had to be satisfied with that—or at least he

seemed to be. Only Hainey, Vandervoort, and one or two others knew of the further preparations Masters was making—preparations as if for something the detective was sure would come.

And it came.

JUST AT DUSK, a man in an overcoat, with felt hat pulled down over his eyes, strolled past the Riverhead jail. He passed twice. The second time he paused a second before the open window of LeNarre's cell. He made a tossing motion with one hand. Several small articles like very tiny pebbles rattled against the bars. Two of the number, however, went through, falling on the floor at the feet of the manacled prisoner.

Inside LeNarre waved through the bars, then swooping on one of the capsules, he tossed it into his mouth. Then he took the pen and paper provided by Masters, sat down, and wrote feverishly for several minutes.

A guard looked in from the corridor, but saw only that the prisoner was writing something, probably a confession. He did not interfere.

Hidden by a clump of bushes, where he had been posted by Masters, Vandervoort watched the incident that took place at the cell window. That some sort of message had passed, the young detective was certain. When the stranger strolled aimlessly on down the street toward a public garage, Vandervoort unobtrusively followed.

Inside the garage was a car, a big fast Packard. In it were two other men, flashily dressed, hard-eyed. The stranger opened the door, started to step in. And at that moment someone stepped in through the garage side-door. It was Hainey, captain of the state troopers. He had a pistol in his hand which was already covering the stranger beside the automobile door.

"Take it easy, guy. Get 'em up!" said the trooper captain quietly.

The stranger whirled, his hand darting toward his pocket. The two men in the car gave startled exclamations. Then they suddenly became motionless, frozen in their places.

In through the front door had come three other troopers, also with pistols drawn. Now others came in through the back.

"You're cornered," said Captain Hainey, eyeing the strangers with grim, expectant eyes. "Coming easy—or *hard?*"

The man beside the Packard looked, shrugged his shoulders. He let his hand fall away from his pocket. "Easy."

MASTERS, WAITING RESTLESSLY upstairs in the jail beside the telephone, lighted endless cigarettes. Then at last the phone tinkled. It was Vandervoort's voice. "Got 'em, Chief—three of 'em! Fellow came by and passed the jail-window twice. Looked like he signalled or something. I tailed him—and we got him and two others in a big car in the garage."

"March 'em over," instructed Masters. "Signalled, did they—?"

"Yeah. Looked like the fellow outside threw pebbles or something."

"Threw pebbles? My God, why didn't you tell me at first—!" Masters threw down the telephone without even waiting to hang the receiver up. He turned toward the stairs, running for all he was worth.

But even as he ran there came, ripping through the night, a wild, piercing cry—a man in utter, unbearable agony!

Down in his cell below, Louis LeNarre was learning at last the full nature of this thing called Death, which he had dealt out so freely to his fellow mortals.

"OLEANDRINE AGAIN, I think!" was Masters' diagnosis, after a brief examination of the body. "This time it was self-administered, however. See, here is another capsule on the floor!"

He bent and picked up a translucent container made to hold two grains of the drug. With this, and with the single sheet of paper he had found waiting for him on the cot, he turned on his heel and went upstairs. This paper, signed with the flourished signature of Louis LeNarre, failed to go into detail the way Masters had hoped it would. But no matter. He had most all the crimes well in mind now.

District Attorney Blodgett regarded the capsule with distaste, after hearing that one like it had killed his important prisoner. Then he read the signed confession, and his brow cleared. After all, this saved him a lot of work, and the necessity for appearance in a long trial where it was by no means sure there would not be a clever defense lawyer to make Blodgett look like a monkey....

The confession read as follows:

I, Louis LeNarre, shot my employer, Chester Braithwaite, with the intention of taking his place as master of Fernycroft and owner of all his possessions. Visiting Southampton with my cousins, the Abeles, last year, I saw Braithwaite for the first time. He was in the water, swimming, and in every way looked so much like me that we could have been taken for twins.

Eventually I planned to kill him and take his place. To do this, it was necessary to murder two people in order to get the position of secretary—a necessary detail in my plans—and then to kill the others, except Braithwaite, to keep anyone from discovering I was not the real Braithwaite. I made my fatal mistake in not having enough nitric acid to consume Braithwaite's body completely, after I had effectively shot him. The only way I could dispose of the remnant at that time was to push it into the plaster in the mold. I was sure I could destroy it afterward, model and all, without any difficulty.

But that damned Jigger Masters became suspicious of me somehow; I could sense it. My chief regret is that my hydrofluoric acid, gas bomb did not get him as I had planned. However, I shall always look forward keenly to meeting him again where I am going! Until then—au revoir!

Louis LeNarre.

"H'm-m-mm. A pleasant sort of note," said Masters, shrugging. "The same monomaniac—murderous to the end."

But the pompous district attorney, Blodgett, banged the desk angrily. "Impossible! Utterly impossible. The man was crazy—no doubt of that. But it wasn't humanly possible for him to commit all those murders!"

"I think I can prove he did," said Masters quietly. "I have said Louis LeNarre was a monomaniac. But that does not mean half-witted, irresponsible. Louis LeNarre's reasoning, his planning, was crafty to the point of brilliancy. In all his mad career, all those frightful days and nights, he made only a few slips. He left almost no clues. Only three or four, and those almost invisible. I'll take them up as I go along.

"In the first place, consider the history of Louis LeNarre. An honor graduate from Amherst, at twenty-eight he was already making ten thousand dollars a year as private secretary to the president of an important company, and with the certainty of going further. Most men of his age would have been satisfied with that—but not Louis LeNarre. He was an egotist—he considered himself above the rest of the world. He cared nothing for girls or women—this we have found out from various witnesses. Power and wealth were the only things he wanted in the world, and he was determined to have them.

"But along with this egotism, there were traces of criminal insanity from the first. Vandervoort, my assistant, investigating his youth, found that he was always a leader among his playmates—and that generally he took the part of the robber or villain in their games.

"In his older days, coming to New York on trips, we find the same tendencies toward evil companions. We have followed his tracks to some of the lowest dives in the city. It is not hard to imagine him planning a criminal organization of several of those he met in those low dives—determined to rise to the power and wealth as men like Capone were supposed to have done."

Masters paused a moment to light a cigarette. "It was an unlucky coincidence probably that brought Braithwaite into LeNarre's sight that day at Southampton. Braithwaite little imagined that merely by swimming past the stranger on shore he had signed his own death warrant—yet that is what it amounted to.

"Not that I think LeNarre planned the murder from the beginning. He merely became interested—learned that his double, Braithwaite, was not only a widower and a sort of recluse, but that he had lately inherited an estate of over six million dollars! That was when LeNarre definitely began scheming.

"At first, I imagine, he probably planned a kidnapping. To do so it would be necessary to plant a member of the ring or organization inside the Fernycroft gates in order to obtain certain needful information. Braithwaite's known idiosyncracy in giving a home to homeless and eccentric scientists offered unusual opportunity. It was easy to get the crippled Peter Unger on the Fernycroft charity list.

"But LeNarre, studying the situation, began to be intrigued with a still more glamorous idea—not to get just part of Braithwaite's fortune, but all of it! His similarity in appearance gave LeNarre the idea of murdering Braithwaite and taking his place. The isolation of Fernycroft, and the eccentricity of its scientist guests, still further tempted LeNarre. First suspicion for any unnatural death that occurred would inevitably fall upon some of the half-mad scientists.

"LeNarre set himself to study the man he intended to impersonate. He learned much through Unger. Some he probably learned through the maid, Lucy Borden, who was boy crazy and easily approached by handsome, well-dressed strangers. LeNarre himself, in disguise, might even have obtained much information from the girl.

"Thus it probably was that LeNarre learned about the skyscraper model contest. He knew then that he must hurry the deed if he intended to do it at all. If Braithwaite won—even if his design received very favorable mention—he would be in the public eye to such an extent that any attempt to impersonate him afterward would have been fatal.

"LeNarre studied Braithwaite more than ever, no doubt practised by the hour; he studied architecture and he studied science. And he laid his plans to remove Sally Holworth so as to obtain the secretarial position himself. He probably also practised up on the art of throwing a knife which we found was one of his proudest accomplishments when a youngster.

"One thing bothered him—Peter Unger was sicker than anyone had guessed. He was mentally as well as physically twisted—and he began to get worse. He began to mutter, to talk—and LeNarre knew it was but a question of time before he would have to get rid of him. The others of his ring—I do not know; probably he never told them his changed plans toward Braithwaite, and they would never have found out—would only have been left wondering dazedly what had become of LeNarre."

MASTERS TOOK OUT of a package which he had brought, a heavy knife wound with fine, strong line. "This is the knife—the death messenger LeNarre chose. Hiding behind the cedars one afternoon he waited until Sally Holworth came along. He hurled the knife into her neck with fatal accuracy—then yanked it out by the line attached to the handle, thus leaving no tracks close to the body for the police to follow. The gathering dark and the crowding around of curious, excited persons, plus the slight snow, eliminated any tracks even further away than the police might have investigated.

"That was the first person successfully removed. But how annoyed the murderer must have been when my assistant,

Barnes, promptly filled in as the new secretary. His elimination was decided upon immediately—by an explosion this time. LeNarre knew chemistry—knew all about the manufacture of explosives—could probably obtain the ingredients unnoticed even if he could not get away with the finished explosive. He rented an old cottage and made his deadly nitroglycerine.

"Hainey's theory is that the nitroglycerine was poured into the battery of the car the murderer knew Barnes would take. I think that it was poured into the radiator, where it would explode at the first jar of the starting engine. Anyway Barnes was so completely eliminated that we never so much as found a little finger even. And LeNarre, suitably disguised as Nathan Ertz, at last secured the position of confidential secretary to Braithwaite—a position where he could watch, listen, obtain the little intimate details of his double that he must know in order to masquerade as Braithwaite even for a few days. For I have no doubt he planned to dispose of Braithwaite's property as quickly as possible and move abroad where there would be less chance of anyone detecting the impersonation.

"Unger had to be disposed of, first. So one night when the secretary, Ertz, was presumably in New York on private business, a stranger claiming to be a newspaper reporter, Lloyd Kendall, came to Riverhead. He interviewed Unger, apparently innocently enough—but on departing, smuggled a little note into Unger's hand. That note we found later in Unger's stomach. There is no doubt in my mind that that note had been loaded with oleandrine, a deadly poison. That, with a brusque admonition to Peter to chew up and swallow the letter afterwards, accomplished the deed. And the third obstructing person was successfully removed from LeNarre's path.

"Braithwaite himself was an easy victim. LeNarre simply waited until the night the plaster for the model skyscraper was poured into the molds—the last possible moment so that no awkward technical points remained to be covered and to lead to questioning—and then LeNarre coldly shot his employer, as he says. Inside that locked laboratory an automatic with a silencer would not be heard.

"Then, with cold-blooded cunning, LeNarre poured nitric acid over the corpse and all its clothes. When the acid had done its work, confined in one of those fume-hooded vats, LeNarre washed it off and then dumped a sack of unslaked lime over what was left. The combined action of those two chemicals was enough to destroy every trace of Braithwaite except a mere wraith of his bony struc-ture. You saw where LeNarre put that, later on the same night the plaster was poured.

"It was one of his few mistakes—and even so would never have been discovered, probably, if he had not let a more definite clue escape him. As he washed the remains of the body, he flushed down the drain a small piece of bone—the second phalanx of Braithwaite's left little finger.

"I found that out in the settling tank—and immediately knew what must have happened. I guessed at the hiding of the other part in the skyscraper plaster—but if there was anything left of any size, I knew that was the only place it could have been hidden.

"It was typical of LeNarre's brilliancy that, for some time after the actual killing, all of us believed that it was Ertz who had disappeared. So thoroughly had LeNarre passed himself off as the actual Braithwaite. This is not greatly to be wondered at, however, as I myself had been acquainted with the real Braithwaite only a few days, and the others were too much preoccupied with their scientific endeavors to be attentive to outside things.

"On one characteristic only did LeNarre fall down—and that, too, struck me at the time as peculiar. Braithwaite had been very fond of Sylvia Reese—even to the point of proposing marriage. LeNarre—posing as Braithwaite—did not so much as mention her even casually—made no effort apparently to see her. More important, he did not know that she had already become engaged to another man, though she told me she had written and told the *real* Braithwaite."

Masters paused a moment, then went on.

"Another contradictory circumstance that caught my attention was when the butler, Martin King, returned from Canada. Braithwaite had always called the butler 'Rex.' Now he suddenly called him 'Martin'—never anything else. It was such a marked change that the butler commented to me about it.

"That was a simple slip—but a bad one for LeNarre. It drew my attention to the most likely explanation: that the reason why Braithwaite no longer addressed the butler the way he had done before was because he *never had seen Martin before.*

"After that, it was simple enough. Static Browne and Dr. Spinelli were removed for the simple reason that they had lived in close contact with the real Braithwaite for a long time—sooner or later they would observe some contradictory little thing in the pseudo-Braithwaite's talk or appearance or actions—would ask him some little but damning question he would be unable to answer.

"The killing of Browne was crude, yet clever. There could be only two possible killers—Dr. Spinelli, and the man then accepted as Braithwaite. And the latter was naked and in a shower bath. The only possible way he could have done the deed was to have climbed over the roof, naked, at a temperature far below freezing, knife Browne from behind the screen; then slip back by way of Spinelli's room, leave the accusing evidence under his bed, and dash back to his own room. It was a performance that would have looked preposterous, incredible—which was just as LeNarre intended it should.

"But clever as he was, LeNarre could not prevent some of the suspicion centering upon him, merely for the reason that he was among those present. He determined to wipe out me and my assistant, whom he had begun to regard as dangerous—and at the same time, if failing to do so, to seemingly prove that it was the missing Ertz who was responsible for all the crimes. If Ertz was the guilty person, then the man accepted as Braithwaite could not possibly be!

"This alibi structure was one of the cleverest of LeNarre's moves. He registered at a hotel in town. He wandered around the Grand Central exhibit, talking to some of the other contestants. The fact that he had come to town in the hearse—with his model building, of course—and that he did not have his car, and that the train schedules made it impossible for him to have ridden by train and still be at the Grand Central when he was—all this would have seemed to establish his innocence beyond all doubt.

"But I had two reporters trace his movements. And we found that, disguised with the wig and horn-rimmed spectacles of Nathan Ertz, he had gone to a drive-it-yourself garage and rented a fast Chrysler Imperial. And the mileage he had to pay for when he returned was enough to have driven all the way to Riverhead and Biskra Harbor and back!"

He sat back, resting.

AT THAT MOMENT Vandervoort and Hainey and the state troopers came in, escorting their captives. The hard-eyed, gray-suited stranger in the lead listened scowlingly to Vandervoort's report, and then turned to Masters as seemingly the one in authority there. "G'wan—you can't arrest us!" he snorted. "We ain't done a thing."

"No?" said Masters quietly. "You don't know anything about any secret society signing itself R-C? You don't know anything about any rosy crosses or waters under the earth or anything like that?"

The gray-suited man started. "What d'ya know about that?" he demanded.

"Oh, aplenty," said Masters, smiling. "You are sure, then, that you don't know anything of any secret society signing itself R-C?"

"Well," said the gray-suited man, "it wasn't us. We didn't have nothing to do with it. It was that other guy's idea—that crazy one's. LeNarre. I told him it was all kid foolishness—them trick words and signs. Him and that Unger nut was the only ones took any stock in it."

"Yes? And you didn't know anything about any plot to kidnap a millionaire named Braithwaite, maybe?" said Masters.

"Sure we did," said the hard-eyed man boldly. "That was another one of LeNarre's crazy ideas. But we never done it. And you can't jail a man for thinking about things. Hell, we couldn't 'a' gone on with that snatch job if we'd wanted to. LeNarre was the only guy had all the inside stuff—and all at once he dropped out on us. We never knew where he was until—until we saw in the papers where he was held for them murders."

"And you never had a thing to do with any of them?"

"Not a thing. We was fools to get tied up with a bunch of nuts like that LeNarre guy and Unger. I'm telling you, you ain't got nothing on us, and you might as well let us go."

"We got enough on you to send you up for a good stretch for the Sullivan act—pistols on all of you," snapped the trooper captain.

But Masters was nodding his head slowly. "It might be hard to prove anything more than that on you after all," he said slowly. "And as for helping LeNarre beat the electric chair I'm not sure it wasn't better justice to have sent him out by the same unpleasant means he used to eliminate Peter Unger. I tell you what: we might let you off light after all— all things considered—if you'll answer one question for us."

"Shoot," invited the gray-suited man.

"What do those letters R-C mean?"

"Them?" the gray-suited man laughed. "The Red Collectors—that was another of that nut LeNarre's ideas. We was going to collect millionaires like Braithwaite—an' then collect money for turnin' 'em loose again. The Red Collectors!" He spat scornfully. "Now ain't that a hell of a name for a bunch of grown men?"

"It is," said Jigger Masters solemnly.

A GIANT IN THE SWIMMING POOL

*Down in That Laboratory Where the Five-
Armed Monsters Whirled, Science Was
Working Out a New Secret and a Man
Was Working Out a Plot of Murder*

1

QUEER MEN, THE Tegarth brothers. One a wheel chair cripple, up there in his fifth-floor office of the factory building. Another down in the basement, working on a secret.

Jigger Masters had finished his preliminary survey of the second floor of the factory, empty now of employees. The detective had discovered nothing at all save the oppressive atmosphere of the place. He caught himself glancing over his shoulder constantly, feeling that eyes were watching him.

Frowning a little, Masters walked to the automatic elevator, which was used only by Lawrence and Elmer Tegarth, who owned the factory. Pressing a button, Masters brought the elevator up to the second floor. He opened the door, which was glass-panelled, stepped out and shut the door again.

Then he shook his head. The sense of impending peril, of being watched breathlessly by an unseen enemy, was stronger. Both of the Tegarth brothers suspected death might be lurking, waiting for them. That was why they had called in Masters, though one of them probably hated the presence of the detective, and would kill swiftly rather than be exposed.

Masters took a small leather case from his left hip

pocket. From this he took a small tool, a wheel glass-cutter, which lay side by side with a folding jimmy.

Four quick, rasping strokes of the cutter, and there was a cracking sound, and then a tinkle of falling glass. Masters thrust one arm through the hole he had made in the glass of the elevator door, and pressed the fifth floor button. With a faint hum the automatic elevator rose and disappeared.

With a shrug of his wide shoulders Masters turned to the staircase, and mounted. Probably a fool precaution, yet that premonition had been strong.

Thump-bump-bump!

The detective halted at the third floor, and twisted his wide mouth in a grimace. The hazel eyes were narrow and cold. That elevator had *not* reached the fifth floor in safety! Somewhere it had stopped, then plunged downward with increasing swiftness. And the hydraulic cushion below must have been tampered with, for the elevator came to rest with a crash that shook the building.

Anyone who had been inside must have been badly hurt—or killed!

Masters ran up to the top floor. There the offices were located. A door opened and Lawrence Tegarth rapidly wheeled his chair out into the little hall where the elevator shaft opened. His face was pale.

"What happened, Mr. Masters?" he cried. "That shock! Was it—the elevator? I would have taken it in a few moments!" Behind him in the office the house phone buzzed. Probably the night watchman on the first floor, or Elmer Tegarth ringing from the basement where the secret laboratory was located.

A strangled cry of horror burst from the lips of Jigger Masters

"Correct!" said Masters grimly, and strode past the elder brother in his wheel chair. He lifted the phone receiver.

"Masters speaking," he said.

"Oh, my heavens!" came a half hysterical voice. "The elevator's fallen. The door down here is wedged some way, so I can't open it! Is my brother inside?"

It was the second brother, Elmer.

"There is nothing to worry about," answered the detective with an edge of irony. "The cage was empty."

He hung up, and faced the man in the wheel chair, who had come back slowly, his long, white hands gripping the rubber-tired wheels of his chair.

"Quickly, before anyone comes," said the detective, closing the office door, "tell me a little more. When you were shot, and suffered this injury to your spine, you were asleep down in the bedchamber near the laboratory?"

"Yes. The shock woke me," said the cripple from between taut lips.

"And except for the night watchman you were alone in the building?"

Lawrence Tegarth hesitated. "I'm not sure," he admitted. "Elmer had been here, but had let himself out hours before. A door was wide open—the east entrance. The watchman found it so when he came down from his two-hour round of the building. He had been up here, probably, at the time of the shot, and had not heard it or seen anyone."

"I see." The detective realized that unless this man were faking his inability to walk, it was out of the question for him to have doctored the elevator. Likewise it was impossible that he had shot himself in the back as he lay down there in bed. There had been no weapon near him. But though he did not say so, it was plain that he did not feel too certain about the loyalty of his own brother.

At that moment Elmer Tegarth burst in, followed by the night watchman, a surly-faced fellow in overalls named Ed Brenner. Brenner held an automatic pistol in his hand, and now shoved it down in the leather holster at his right hip. Elmer turned to the man.

"All right, you can go back down. Try to pry open that elevator door with a crowbar, and see how that smash happened."

With a grunt, Ed Brenner turned and shuffled away. Elmer Tegarth closed the office door.

"Thank God you're all right, Larry!" he breathed then, mopping his forehead. "I was sure something had happened to you."

JIGGER MASTERS WAS troubled, and not a little angry.

The Tegarth factory was devoted to the manufacture of antiseptics, plant sprays, insect powders and the like. But there was something more—these secret experiments. They would not divulge that.

All of the basement not used for the storage of raw materials and chemicals ready for shipment, he had found out, was given over to the private use of the Tegarth brothers. There was a tiny swimming pool, shower and locker room, a bedroom containing two single beds. Here either or both of the brothers had been accustomed to sleep, nights they worked late on their experiments.

The big laboratory adjoined this room. And Masters had been told that not even he would be admitted to the laboratory. They had been working for more than a year on some process or substance which they thought would make them huge fortunes. It could not be patented, they said, so it had been kept a profound secret in the brains of just the two of them.

"You may be handicapping me too greatly," the detective said. "You tell me that you possess a valuable secret; that no one else in the world guesses it. There is peril to you, and now to me, since I am investigating the happenings here. At first blush I'd say that laboratory and its secret *must* have something to do with it!"

"But we are resolved—" began Lawrence Tegarth.

He got no further. From somewhere far below came a quake and muffled thunder—an explosion! The windows rattled and even the floor of cement and tile heaved underfoot.

"A bomb—in the lab!" yelled Elmer Tegarth.

In the mind of Jigger Masters, as he flew downstairs,

was one terse summary. Both these men who seemed to suspect each other, had been in his presence. And the night watchman, Brenner, no matter how fast he ran down the steps, could not have reached the basement before that explosion occurred.

Who then could have caused it?

There was no question now about letting Masters view the laboratory. The explosion had taken place there, and as far as most of the apparatus was concerned, the place was a wreck.

Masters and Ed Brenner, both with ready weapons, were first to push in past the wreckage of the steel door which had been buckled on its hinges.

"You go out and look for signs of someone!" bade Masters crisply. "No one stayed in here while *that* happened! It smells like a crude bomb—black powder…"

Scowling and with bad grace, Ed Brenner obeyed. He seemed to be a rather dumb, ill-natured specimen, and Masters preferred him out of the way.

Elmer Tegarth, the younger, fair-haired brother, joined the detective. He said that Lawrence had phoned for the two servants to come in his car and take him home. He would wait long enough only to hear what had happened in the basement. Though he was getting better gradually, the spine injury forced him to be cautious, and undergo as little strain as possible.

Masters and young Tegarth looked about the wrecked laboratory, full of the smoke and dust of the explosion.

"What a narrow escape!" muttered Elmer. "If I hadn't run up after hearing from you, Mr. Masters, I'd have been killed sure as fate!"

"Looks that way," agreed the detective, reserving his decision. Two narrow escapes by both of the brothers, and all within a matter of minutes… He went ahead with a quick examination of the laboratory.

2

ON CLOSE INSPECTION the damage was not as great as might have been imagined. On one side and at one end the heavy machinery remained with little mark. As the smoke gradually thinned, Masters looked about him with the slight chill of awe most men feel when facing monstrous and inexplicable machinery.

There were eight huge tanks like railway oil tankers without the trucks, along the right-hand wall. Beside them were four stubby-armed, gigantic things, each with five arms like elongated barrels.

Elmer Tegarth shook his head decidedly and refused to say anything about the five-armed giants. He did answer one question concerning the big tanks, though. They did not contain gas or anything explosive. They were all filled with an inert liquid, he said.

"And nobody but you and your brother has been in here? Not ever?" demanded Masters.

"No—except when this machinery was installed, of course. Then there were workmen. And five or six times when we had connections of piping to make, we called on Ed Brenner. He used to be assistant engineer in a skyscraper in New York, before the depression. He's good at plumbing and pipe-fitting—things like that. Otherwise he's too dumb to know his eye from his elbow... I hear voices out there. That will be Larry. The servants are taking him home. I'll just go tell him what we've found. Then I think I'll take a plunge in the pool and go home, too. I'm rather shaken, and tired. You'll sleep there in the chamber next door. Call on Ed Brenner for anything you want. He makes a round of the building every two hours…"

Masters nodded. He was glad to have a chance to look more thoroughly into this laboratory. Right or wrong, he felt that the secret of the bombing and of the attempt on the life of Lawrence—not to speak of the doctored elevator—would have its explanation here, if only he were able to read it.

Immediately he turned back to the machinery, a slight frown on his forehead. The bomb had been exploded underneath the center table, the one at which Elmer Tegarth did much of his work.

He made a close examination to determine the focal point of explosion. There had been no fake about the destructiveness of the bomb. If the maker of the bomb had used tri-nitrotoluol instead of black powder, there would have been little but rubbish left of the entire factory building!

That in no way exonerated Elmer Tegarth. It would have been almost too simple for a chemist to have made such a bomb, then lit a short fuse to burn while he went upstairs.

Masters went to the end of the room where he saw a wall cupboard. Opening this, he looked at a set of switches. He reached in and opened one that was closed. All the lights went out. He pushed it closed and reached for another which had been standing open.

A *whirr* and rush of air at the height of his head made

him jerk about, the instant that contact was made. Then he grinned. Those five-armed monsters had sprung to life! The arms were whirling horizontally at a speed too great for the eye to follow!

"Well, I remember what you must be, now," the detective muttered. The machines were giant centrifuges, whirling contrivances for separating liquids of unequal weight—or for separating solids from liquids. The only such machines he had seen before had been the tiny ones. These barrel-armed dervishes could do the same thing with hundreds of gallons of liquid, that the little centrifuges did with tens of cubic centimeters…

Opening the switch, Masters stepped past the whirling giants at a respectful distance. He picked up a long-handled spanner wrench from the floor litter, and walked over to the first pair of the eight huge tanks. He swung the wrench and struck the belly of the tank a resounding blow.

A bright metallic *clang!* answered him!

Drawing a deep breath, he stepped along, striking each of the eight tanks. In every case there came that *clang!* and hollow booming!

In spite of what the younger Tegarth had said—that these receptacles were filled with an inert liquid—Masters knew that *every one of them was dry and empty!*

Was Tegarth himself unaware of the fact, after just working for hours in this very room?

One thing was growing to certainty in Masters' mind. The chemical secret, the mystery of this laboratory, was linked up closely with the attempted murders.

At that moment Ed Brenner burst in, scowling savagely. "What the hell's goin' on here now?" he demanded in a raucous, suspicious voice. "Mr. Tegarth, he don't allow nobody to monkey! You stop hammerin' or I'll call him—"

"Taking his swim, is he?" asked Masters. "Well, let him finish. Then I'll call him myself. Look here, Brenner, you are to help me, not make my job harder. What have you found out in regard to that elevator?"

The watchman shrugged his heavy shoulders. "Oh, it was cooked to kill somebody, all right," he snarled. "The water was gone out of the hydraulic cushion down below."

"But how did it fall in the first place?"

"The cables was filed through. There are four of 'em. The fella who did it must of cut all but one small wire in each one. Then when that part came to the wheels up above, why, down come the cage, zowie!"

The detective dismissed Brenner. Then instantly he got down on his hands and knees. For half a minute he had been conscious of a faint, peculiar sound, and had been puzzling over its origin. It seemed at first to be all about him as he stood between the tanks. The centrifuges now were run down and quiet. The sound was steady, and at first the detective could not find just where it seemed strongest.

Then after minutes of search and intent listening, he traced it to the vent pipe below the tanks. But the tanks themselves had been empty. What then could be flowing steadily?

Why, the swimming pool, of course! It probably drained out through the same sewer main, and that accounted for the murmur coming back through the vent pipe and the tanks. He would hurry to make sure, and to ask some questions of Elmer Tegarth as the latter dressed.

But the moment he switched on the lights and entered

the steamy natatorium, however, a strangled cry of horror burst from the lips of Jigger Masters.

The swimming tank was empty of water. Face down near the deep end, arms outspread, lay the naked body of Elmer Tegarth!

IN THE FLASH of an instant, as he climbed down into the tank, Masters realized this was no accident such as has occurred so often, when a man, half blind from a shower, dashes in and dives—before noticing the tank is empty—breaking his neck.

This tank had been full, and just now had been drained by someone.

In quick examination of the body Masters found no broken bones at all, not even a bad bruise. What could have happened?

With a yell for help from Ed Brenner, Masters lifted the body, hitched it to one shoulder, and managed to climb the ladder out of the pool. In the locker room he dumped Tegarth face downward across the central bench between the lockers, and kneeled on his shoulder blades.

Water gushed out of the man's lungs.

Quick as thought Masters reached up to a container of lily cups above the wash basins, snatching out two. Then he pressed again on Tegarth's chest, and filled both cups as the water spilled out of the victim's mouth.

Might be poison of some kind, as well as drowning… Masters set the two full cups atop one of the lockers, and set about furiously the task of administering artificial respiration.

Three minutes passed. Nothing happened to show Tegarth was alive. The watchman had not appeared. Probably he was up on one of the higher floors. Masters drew his pistol and fired three shots into the wooden door.

Then the watchman appeared, breathless. "Wh-what's happened?" he gasped.

"Call the police ambulance with a pulmotor! Got that? A pulmotor! This man's drowned, but maybe not dead. Hurry!"

The watchman turned, and walked away without haste. A minute later Masters heard his snarling voice in the corridor as he telephoned.

With commendable promptitude the ambulance squad with two policemen appeared, and Masters gave over what looked like a useless job. But there was no telling. Men had been resuscitated after a much longer period of apparent death…

Masters took the pair of policemen to one side, and gave them low-voiced instructions which made them stare— and then turn around and look menacingly at the figure of Ed Brenner, who leaned against a locker.

Brenner caught the look, and started to sidle out of the room. They stopped him, and brought him back to the far end, where they persuaded him to sit down. There they waited, paying no attention to his surly protests.

There was nothing Masters could do to help Tegarth now. He was in expert hands. So the detective, his mind on those lily cups, hurried around the L corridor to the laboratory. There he picked up a dented beaker which looked like silver, and washed it thoroughly. The beaker was platinum, one used in handling substances which will eat their way through glass.

Back in the locker room he lifted down one of the flexible cups, and was about to pour it into the beaker, when he noted something queer. The cup seemed far heavier than it should.

A thrill coursed through Masters. He knew—or suspected strongly—a whole lot about this business now!

Since the bottom of the flimsy container was beginning to bulge, he poured it hurriedly into the beaker. Then he ran for another lily cup, and filled it with plain water at the basin faucet. Returning, he reached down the second of the cups he had filled with the water from Tegarth's lungs.

This was nearly twice as heavy as the lily cup filled with plain water at the faucet!

Masters poured in the second bulging cup of water from Tegarth's lungs, into the beaker, then took that latter container out of the room, covered it, and hid it. It was evidence of something mighty like murder!

Striding back into the room of the pool, he looked about questioningly. This might have been done by hand, but he doubted it. Well—there it was—

He strode down to the foot of the rubber-carpeted ladder which rose to the pair of diving platforms. Here was an oblong disc of gray rubber, attached by a small chain to a ring on the side of the pool near the top. The disc had been placed out of sight under the ladder, but Masters drew it forth by the chain. And then he smiled grimly.

That gray disc of rubber was dry on both sides! It could not have been in place at the bottom of the tank for many hours!

Of course something else must have been in its place, or else the big drain through which the tank was emptied would have let out the water as fast as it flowed in…

Down the chromium ladder to the floor of the tank at the deep end. There Jigger bent, examining the wide oblong aperture where the water escaped. He grunted satisfaction at finding there was a grille two inches beneath the surface, probably put there to keep the drain from being clogged.

On this grille were three irregular fragments of some thin, whitish granular substance. Masters lifted them out carefully, and wrapped them in a silk handkerchief. Since this factory was devoted to the manufacture of antiseptics and plant sprays, he could guess well enough the nature of this substance.

His face was grim as he climbed the ladder. He had evidence of deliberate murder, though it might be difficult to cinch the crime on the killer himself.

3

BUT IT WAS not murder!

As Jigger Masters reached the door of the locker room, his heart leaped. Elmer Tegarth was breathing. More than that, he was hunched up on the floor, nauseated, and groaning from somewhere deep down near his knee-caps.

"Will he live?" cried Jigger.

"Sure he'll live—now. You got us just in time, Mr. Masters," replied one of the white-coated ambulance men. "In ten or fifteen minutes we'll take him on a stretcher. A day or two in the hospital will be what he wants right now."

With the excitement of the patient's recovery, the two policemen had left Ed Brenner. He, too, had crowded close to have a look at the man so miraculously returned from the grave. But now with the entrance of Jigger Masters, the watchman unobtrusively started to edge out of the room.

Masters caught him by the elbows.

"We want you right here, Ed Brenner," he said sternly. "There's a little matter of four attempted murders against you."

"What the hell you talkin' about? He's all right, ain't he?" snarled the man. I ain't done nothin'."

"I want you to come back here—and let me clean your fingernails right now!" snapped Masters. "If there should

be a little white stuff there—calcium chloride, for a guess—
I'd—"

He got no further. With a yell of rage, Ed Brenner
hunched his muscled shoulders and broke away from the
retaining grasp. He swung about, evil face contorted, drawing his pistol and mouthing hate against this detective who
had come in unexpectedly to spoil his careful coup.

Jigger Masters had not expected quite this. He did not
have time to draw his own weapon. Instead he lunged
forward with a straight right punch to the jaw, following this with a left to the heart which did not connect as
solidly, and then stepping fast to hammer his man back
through the doorway with piston-like body punches aimed
to disable.

The watchman's pistol exploded once. Back in the room
a heavy-set policeman, shocked out of his dumb amaze-
ment, sat down suddenly, clasping his foot and swearing
with earnest anger.

That was nearly all. Masters hit the staggering Brenner
twice more. The watchman went backward through the
doorway, seemed to catch his heel, and screamed as he fell
over into the vacancy of the empty tank.

Down there nine feet, he struck with his head twisted
sidewise. There was an audible crunch, and then he rolled
down a foot and lay still.

Masters peered over at him, then arose to confront the
second policeman. "That man won't try to murder anyone
else," he said gravely. "I can't say that I'm sorry!"

In Brenner's quarters they found a length of steam pipe.
In it lay a can half full of black powder such as must have
been used in the laboratory bomb.

Also a second pistol was hidden there. This was of .38 caliber, probably the weapon with which Lawrence Tegarth had been shot.

This evidence satisfied the police, clearing up the mystery on their records. Masters had no difficulty then, by granting the police full credit, in persuading them to say nothing of these last happenings. The case was officially closed as a shooting that had been solved, and a would-be murderer accidentally killed while attempting to escape arrest.

"THAT LETS YOU two keep your secret," smiled Masters, when two days later he was called by the brothers Tegarth. Elmer had fully recovered from his near drowning; and the crippled Lawrence appeared happier than he had been in months.

"Your Ed Brenner was really a steam engineer out of luck," said Masters. "Nights when you two were down in the laboratory working on your experiments—and talking, no doubt—he overheard. He knew water, if not quite so much about murder. And your experiments concerned a peculiar kind of water."

"Yes, that's true," Larry admitted gravely. "Go on."

"It's the new *heavy water*, of course," nodded Masters. "Professor Urey of Columbia and Professor Taylor of Princeton have been experimenting with it. You two men discovered how to make it in large quantity—probably by using your big centrifuges.

"Since you have this kind of business anyway, I suggest you were trying to use heavy water in the manufacture of a new, cheap antiseptic spray. Microscopic plant and animal life cannot exist, of course, in heavy water as it does in ordinary water...."

"Correct as hell. Go on with our secret—as you call it!" said Elmer grimly.

"Well, that's nearly all. Brenner was here all the time and had plenty opportunity to arrange bombs, doctor the mechanism of elevators, and so on.

"He simply drained out the ordinary water from the swimming tank, then filled the tank with your heavy water from those eight storage tanks in the next room—after putting in that slowly soluble plug of calcium chloride, instead of the usual tank plug of gray rubber.

"That meant that after a time the tank would drain dry, without having to be manipulated in any way.

"Brenner knew about your habits, Mr. Tegarth. Probably you always started your swim with a high dive." Elmer nodded. "The effect of diving into a tank of heavy water is much the same as diving into a tank full of sand. You stunned yourself, then started to drown."

"My neck is still stiff and sore," grinned Elmer.

"So then that's all. Brenner wanted the secret of your heavy water for himself; but your secret is safe."

"It *will* be safe, I think, if you will agree to this proposal," said Lawrence dryly, a twinkle in his dark eyes. "We have never inquired about your charges, Mr. Masters. But now is the time to consider them. Will you take your fee in stock of this company? Say, $5,000 worth of stock at par? It is worth a small premium now, I believe, and if this heavy water disinfectant is a success—"

"Thank you!" smiled Jigger Masters. "I'll be mighty glad to gamble in secrets with you both!"

www.ingramcontent.com/pod-product-compliance
Lightning Source LLC
Chambersburg PA
CBHW072355030726

47505CB00014B/1838

* 9 7 8 1 6 1 8 2 7 8 5 9 3 *